“She’s just so…little.”

Seeing Caroline like this—vulnerable, scared—made Seth want to wrap her in his arms and tell her she didn’t need to worry. That he was right here. He wouldn’t let anything happen to Nina.

But he couldn’t. Because he had no plans to be part of her life. And even if he did, he couldn’t prevent anything happening to Nina any more than she could.

“Mommy?” Nina appeared in the archway. Spud trailed behind her. “Mr. Hudson!”

She raced to where he sat and beamed up at him.

“Hey there, Nina.”

“Why are you here?”

“Your mom and I thought you might like to go to the park and walk Spud on the leash.”

“Really? Yay! I get to hold the leash?”

“You sure do.” His heart was dissolving into mush. First Caroline’s honesty had worn down his resistance to being her friend, and now this cutie was acting like he was her hero for letting her walk Spud on a leash.

He never should have gotten involved with these two.

Jill Kemerer writes novels with love, humor and faith. Besides spoiling her mini dachshund and keeping up with her busy kids, Jill reads stacks of books, lives for her morning coffee and gushes over fluffy animals. She resides in Ohio with her husband and two children. Jill loves connecting with readers, so please visit her website, jillkemerer.com, or contact her at PO Box 2802, Whitehouse, OH 43571.

Books by Jill Kemerer

Love Inspired

Wyoming Inheritance

The Rancher's Mistletoe Baby
A K-9 to Reunite Them

Wyoming Legacies

The Cowboy's Christmas Compromise
United by the Twins
Training the K-9 Companion
The Cowboy's Christmas Treasures
The Cowboy's Easter Surprise
His New Companion

Wyoming Ranchers

The Prodigal's Holiday Hope
A Cowboy to Rely On
Guarding His Secret
The Mistletoe Favor
Depending on the Cowboy
The Cowboy's Little Secret

Visit the Author Profile page at LoveInspired.com for more titles.

A K-9 TO REUNITE THEM

JILL KEMERER

MIX
Paper | Supporting responsible forestry
FSC® C021394

ISBN-13: 978-1-335-62146-7

A K-9 to Reunite Them

For questions and comments about the quality of this book, please contact us at CustomerService@Harlequin.com.

Love Inspired
22 Adelaide St. West, 41st Floor
Toronto, Ontario M5H 4E3, Canada
www.LoveInspired.com

HarperCollins Publishers
Macken House, 39/40 Mayor Street Upper,
Dublin 1, D01 C9W8, Ireland
www.HarperCollins.com

Printed in Lithuania

The other disciples therefore said unto him,
We have seen the Lord. But he said unto them,
Except I shall see in his hands the print of the nails,
and put my finger into the print of the nails, and
thrust my hand into his side, I will not believe.

Jesus saith unto him, Thomas, because thou hast
seen me, thou hast believed: blessed are they that
have not seen, and yet have believed.

—*John* 20:25, 29

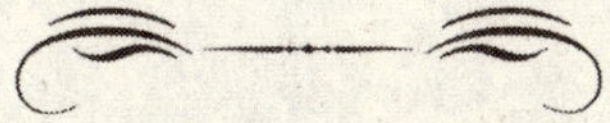

For all the amazing people who dedicate their lives to training service dogs. Thank you.

Chapter One

Was he ready to say goodbye to a decade of training service dogs?

Seth Hudson tuned out his siblings and cousins—affectionately referred to as "the squad"—as they trickled to the driveway after touring the house and pole barn on two acres near the outskirts of Fairwood, Wyoming. If the squad approved, Hudson Ranch Incorporated would purchase the property for him to open a dog-boarding center. He'd spent a good chunk of time putting together a business plan and scoping out available properties. Yesterday, he'd finally presented the business plan to the squad.

"You're not seriously giving up training medical alert dogs, are you?" Kylie, his younger sister, who'd recently turned twenty-eight, stared at him with concern. They'd always had a strong bond, and over the years she'd helped him take care of dogs on weekends many times.

"Yeah, I am. It's time." A warm breeze tickled his bare arms. Perfect weather for late May—a prelude to summer. The green leaves of a tall oak rustled above the gravel drive. His straw cowboy hat shaded his eyes as the brilliant blue sky spread out before him.

Since moving to his cabin on Hudson Ranch in February, Seth had been trying to figure out what he wanted to do with his life. After over a decade of working for a national company in

Dallas, he'd become highly skilled at training service dogs. But the travel was killing him, and he was ready to put down some roots—here, with his best friends, who happened to be family.

Last fall, the six of them had inherited their grandfather's ranch and become equal partners in the company. While the cattle operation was the main focus, they were each given the opportunity to run a business of their choosing as long as the other five approved.

He just needed them to vote yes and the dog-boarding center would become reality.

"But it's your passion." Kylie's eyebrows drew together.

"I'll still offer training," Seth reassured her. "Obedience. Puppy skills. That sort of thing." He tried not to take her concerns personally. He appreciated the fact she worried about him, and, to be fair, he had misgivings about switching careers, too. But something had to change or he'd end up burned out. Unfulfilled.

Maybe he already was.

"Why didn't you say anything to me about this earlier?" Kylie's long, dark brown hair with reddish-brown streaks trailed down her back, the ends lifting in the breeze.

"I wasn't sure I wanted to go through with it. Didn't want to ruffle any feathers until I'd made up my mind." A hawk soared overhead. This place was so peaceful. He could see himself living here.

"But I would have helped you—"

"I know." He trusted his sister. But he'd been burned by two other women—women who should have given him the benefit of the doubt but chose to believe the worst about him instead. Asking anyone for an opinion about something this life-changing hadn't seemed wise. "I needed to figure things out for myself."

His older brother, Hayden, joined them. "I like the property. It's a good spot for dog boarding. Close to town, but not so close people will get upset at barking." At thirty-two, Hayden often seemed twenty years older. He'd been examining the foundation of the three-bedroom house built in the '70s. The large pole barn and other outbuildings had been added later. "Are you sure you want to quit your job? I thought you loved training canines."

Maybe Seth *should* have told the squad about the idea before springing the business plan on them yesterday. But what if they'd tried to talk him out of it?

"I'm sure." Seth nodded. It was only natural they had questions. "I can't keep traveling so much. I want to sleep in my own bed every night and watch football and hunt and hang out with you guys."

"I like the sound of that." Cooper, the cousin closest in age to him—they were both thirty—and Seth's best friend, came up to them. "Why not train service dogs here? You'll have the space."

Seth had briefly considered it, but it wouldn't solve his main problem. "I'd still have to travel to teach the new owners how to handle the dogs. No more. I need a life. A real life."

"I can help you plan the layout of the center." Meena, his youngest cousin—the same age and best friends with Kylie—approached. Her sparkling blue eyes said she approved of his choice. At least one of them did.

"I think we've seen everything." His cousin Brody, the CEO of Hudson Ranch Incorporated and the eldest of the squad, came over and stood next to Kylie. "From what you included in the business plan, your vision for the center—the income projections, how many dogs you anticipate housing, the obedience training you'll offer, even potential growth with an on-site grooming business—is impressive."

Seth nodded his thanks, surprised at how much Brody's praise meant to him. The squad had been supportive of him his entire life. He probably should have trusted them with his plans before now.

"The price is competitive," Brody said. "I think it's a good investment for Hudson Ranch Inc. Should we head to the lodge to vote?"

Their monthly meetings were usually held at the lodge—the main house on the ranch.

"Can we do it here?" Meena asked. "I have to stop by the library before it closes."

No one objected. Meena passed around a notepad and pen, and Hayden collected the votes in his hat. Brody tallied them right there in the driveway.

"It's unanimous." Brody beamed. "Seth, looks like we're putting an offer on this place. If they accept, you'll need to get estimates from local contractors. From what you outlined in the business plan and after seeing this place for myself, we should be able to approve most of the renovations."

"Barring any major issues," Hayden added ominously. Seth was used to his brother pointing out potential problems. It was in his blood to anticipate the worst-case scenario.

Brody gave Hayden a pointed stare as everyone began to congratulate Seth.

"I'm so happy for you!" Meena hugged him. Cooper brought him in for a half embrace. Brody and Hayden congratulated him, too. The four of them headed to their vehicles, and Meena turned around. "We'll see you back at the lodge. Sonny's grilling steaks."

Seth could go for a steak, especially one grilled by the lodge's full-time chef, Sonny Armstrong, who had years of experience working for prestigious restaurants.

As the others drove away, Kylie hung back.

"Hey, Kylie, I didn't mean to hurt your feelings. I needed to work everything out on my own before telling you guys."

"I guess I can understand that."

"Why don't you help me name this place?" He elbowed her side as they headed to her car.

"Really?"

"Yeah. Of course."

"Okay. Perfect Puppy? Hudson's Hounds?" Her eyes twinkled as she gave him a sideways glance. "Rover Resort?"

"Keep trying."

"Doggy Motel."

"No." Seth opened the driver's side door for her. "You seriously need to move to Fairwood."

"I know." She sighed. "I've got a few months left on my lease. I just don't know what I'll do here." Kylie was a certified nursing assistant in Cheyenne. She and Cooper were the only ones who hadn't relocated to the ranch, but Cooper was moving back in a couple of weeks. All six of them had their own cabins. Their wealthy grandmother had had them built not far from the lodge years ago before she died.

"You'll figure it out," Seth said.

"I hope so." She got into the car and gave him a wave. As soon as she'd driven away, Seth circled to take in the property. For the first time, he allowed himself to believe his life really was going to change for the better. He might not be training service dogs, but he'd still be working with dogs. Giving them a safe place to stay while their owners were out of town. Teaching people how to make their dogs obey them. He might even start breeding dogs.

Whistling, he strolled to his truck, pausing as a silver minivan turned into the drive. He hoped it wasn't someone else interested in buying the place. The house had been unoccupied for two months. He'd be surprised if there ended up being any competition for it.

A woman got out of the minivan. He froze. It wasn't just any woman.

Caroline Bright strode his way.

Seth straightened, widening his stance, and lifted his chin. He hadn't seen Caroline in ten—no, twelve—years. Not since the day of her mother's funeral.

Caroline had been his best friend the summer after he graduated from high school. And she'd destroyed their relationship. She'd devastated him. He'd been halfway in love with her at the time.

Whatever she had to say, he didn't want to hear it.

Nothing would spoil his new life here. She'd already ruined his life once. She wouldn't do it again—not if he had anything to say about it.

She'd picked the wrong day for heels.

If stalking Seth Hudson wasn't an act of desperation, Caroline Bright didn't know what was. She'd driven past this house four times until she was certain only Seth remained. For a minute there, she'd feared he'd drive away before she could talk to him. But his truck was still parked in the drive.

As she wobbled across the gravel in shoes not meant for uneven ground, she debated the wisdom of coming. How could she have the audacity to ask Seth to help her?

Because he was the only person qualified to do what she needed.

Earlier, on a break from her new job as a legal assistant for Thompson Law in downtown Fairwood, she'd stopped into Sit and Sip Coffee for a coffee to go when she'd overheard local real estate agent Jan Track say that Seth and his family were touring this property today. Caroline's dad had told her all about how the six cousins had inherited their grandfather's ranch. She hadn't run into any of them in the two weeks she'd been living here. For that she was grateful.

She'd taken a blowtorch to her relationship with Seth years ago and had regretted it ever since.

Seth's brown eyes flared with something dangerous as she came to a halt before him. If she didn't know he worked with service dogs, she'd have mistaken him for a cowboy. The short-sleeved shirt, jeans, cowboy boots and hat—not to mention his toned muscles—practically shouted he didn't have a desk job.

"Caroline." The word was flat. But his voice brought back a slew of memories and emotions. She could not think about them now.

"Hi, Seth." She plastered on a smile, hoping they could be civil. "I heard you moved to your grandparents' ranch."

"I did." He didn't twitch. Didn't blink.

"I understand you train service dogs."

Nothing.

She didn't get intimated easily, but this man clearly held a grudge. A bead of sweat formed at her temple. She refused to brush it away.

"Look, I know I'm the last person who should ask you for a favor." She searched his expression, and all she got was ice, maybe granite. She forged ahead anyhow. "But will you hear me out?"

He considered her for a few beats as the bead of sweat traveled down the side of her face. This time she did brush it away.

"A favor?" No emotion came through. "What do you want?"

"You're able to train medical alert dogs, right?" She'd done enough research to know he'd been training them for years.

"Yes." He crossed his arms over his chest. Not a good sign.

"What about diabetic alert dogs?"

"What about them?"

"Do you train them?"

"Yes."

"I need you to train one for me." As soon as the words left her mouth, she wanted to take them back. She shouldn't have blurted out her request, especially not with him in this mood. The fine art of negotiation was currently lost on her.

"You're diabetic?" His face screwed up in confusion.

"No." She shook her head. She was going about this all wrong. "Not me. My daughter."

The way his eyes widened? She'd say she shocked him.

"I didn't realize you were married."

"I'm not."

He looked like he wanted to ask for more information, but he didn't say a word.

"Nina is my five-year-old daughter. Ten months ago, she was diagnosed with type 1 diabetes. We're managing it as well as we can. She recently got a continuous glucose monitor—a CGM—and the doctors are pleased with how it's going."

"Why does she need a dog? Sounds like you've got everything under control."

She could practically hear the unspoken *as usual*. She would not bristle. She'd be mature. This was for Nina.

"You never really have type 1 diabetes under control. The CGM has glitched a few times. Nina knows she has to keep the reader with her, but she's a kid. She's not perfect. Has she forgotten it in the house to play in the backyard? Yes. But she's only done that twice." She should stop talking. Shouldn't give him any reason to turn her down. "I get the readings and alarms on my phone, but with the spotty cell service around here, I don't always get notifications, especially not while I'm at work."

"Who takes care of her?"

"Happy Time Daycare." Caroline stared down at her heels, then sighed and met his eyes. "I wake up at night worried about her glucose levels. She's starting school this fall. What if…?" She shook her head. "I need a backup plan. *She* needs a backup plan."

The familiar panic strangled her. It had been her companion since before Nina was diagnosed. Caroline could keep her composure through most of the day, only to descend into a torture session of what-ifs when she collapsed into bed at night.

What if Nina falls into a diabetic coma during the night and I can't get her to the hospital in time? What if the daycare center misses the reader's alarm and doesn't give her juice or hard candies? What if they forget to give her the insulin shot before lunch? What if...?

She realized Seth was watching her.

"I don't usually pair small children with service dogs." His closed-off expression didn't surprise her. Nor did his words.

She let out a snort. Like she hadn't heard that from the four other dog trainers she'd contacted. Seth truly was her last resort. What could she say to convince him?

He cocked his head to the side. "Little kids aren't always developmentally ready for the commitment. They don't understand how to handle service dogs. They want to play with the dog, run around with it, and it interferes with the dog's ability to alert them to symptoms. Most kids simply don't have the maturity to take on the responsibility."

Each word he uttered activated the emotions clogging her throat. She balled her hands into fists by her sides.

She'd heard it all. She didn't want to hear it again.

"Nina is different." Her voice was low, controlled. "She can handle the responsibility."

"Look, I'm not training service dogs anymore."

"Could you make an exception? At least meet Nina before saying no?" She couldn't—wouldn't—accept no for an answer. Her daughter's health was too important. And she didn't want to know why he wasn't training dogs anymore. Not if it meant she had to give up on this quest.

After what felt like an hour, Seth spoke. "I'll make a few calls. See if there are any potential dogs. But I wouldn't get your hopes up."

Too late. Her hopes were already up.

"Thank you, Seth." She had the grace to lower her gaze. He owed her nothing. Less than nothing. If anything, she owed him. "I'm sorry, you know, about what happened." She wouldn't ruin the moment by stirring up the past. "Maybe the fact we both moved to Fairwood recently is God's providence."

"Don't."

"What?"

"Don't act like we can pick up where we left off."

"I'm not—"

"We might both live in this town, but we're never going to be friends." His jaw shifted, and his eyes stormed. "I'll be civil. I'll even call around to see if any dogs are available. But that's as far as it will ever go between you and me."

She swallowed the pain his words brought. "I don't need to be friends. I need my daughter to be safe. Please find a dog for her."

"I can't promise that. You might not get one."

Caroline wasn't ready to face that possibility. "Thank you for listening. Thank you for trying. Here's my number. Let me know what you find out." She handed him a note with her number and address on it, then turned to leave.

"Hey, Caroline?" She halted, looking over her shoulder. "Your last name is still Bright?"

"It's still Bright." Let him do what he wanted with that information. She'd never been married. Only a handful of people knew the truth about Nina, and she planned on keeping it that way. She'd tell her daughter she was adopted on her terms. For the moment, she had a million other things to worry about.

She could only pray God would soften Seth's heart and be the answer to her prayer.

Chapter Two

Seth was officially unemployed, and it felt great. He couldn't remember the last time he'd had an extended break from traveling. One week ago, the squad had voted yes on purchasing the property, and the owner had accepted the offer. The closing would be in two weeks. He'd gotten permission from the owner to bring out a contractor today. He had a good feeling about Hector Martin. They'd spent the past two hours going over all the changes that needed to be made. Hector was currently taking a call at the other end of the pole barn while Seth poked around a room up front. Way too small for an office.

"Hey, Liverwurst. I was wondering where you went." Seth bent to pet his American foxhound. The three-year-old dog had been his constant companion since being weaned at eight weeks old. He couldn't imagine life without the affectionate, curious, energetic dog. Liverwurst excelled at setting new dog trainees at ease, which made Seth's job—former job—easier. "I hope you like this place. We're going to be spending a lot of time here, buddy."

Meena had already used her interior design skills to render a virtual model of the house renovations, mostly cosmetic. New flooring, new appliances and a paint job. He trusted her to make the house comfortable and dog-friendly. She'd also mocked up a layout for the pole barn to accommodate boarding the dogs and to allow space for exercise and training. Hector had made a few practical suggestions, but overall, her design fit Seth's vision.

The only downside about buying this place was that Seth wouldn't be living on the ranch with the squad anymore. Sure, they each had privacy in their own cabins, but he'd been enjoying eating breakfast and supper with them at the lodge over the past months whenever he wasn't traveling. At least he could stay on the ranch until this place was ready for customers.

Summer with the squad. Just like old times. Except the final old time had been devastating. All because of Caroline.

For the past week he'd tried to purge her from his mind, but the beautiful woman proved impossible not to think about. She'd always been stunning. With her long, dark brown hair, dark brown eyes, high cheekbones and full lips, she made heads turn. Add that to her get-things-done personality and he could be forgiven for having her on his mind far too often this week.

He couldn't help being attracted to her, but he *could* prevent himself from acting on it.

"Where were we?" Hector approached, sliding his phone in his pocket, and studied the clipboard. "Did you make a decision about restrooms?"

"Yes, I have." Seth shook away thoughts of Caroline. "Let's go with two bathrooms next to the break room." He planned on hiring a small staff to help take care of the dogs while he managed the place.

"How big do you want the break room?"

"What do you suggest?" After going back and forth about the size, they discussed kennels, play areas, new lighting, doggy cams and expanding the office. Then they headed outside to measure areas to fence in for outdoor playtime.

"I want a perimeter fence installed around this portion of the property, too." Seth extended his finger. "That way if a dog manages to dig under one fence and escape, it won't be able to leave the property."

"Smart thinking."

When they finished, Seth accompanied Hector to his truck and shook his hand.

"I'll be in touch soon with the estimate," Hector said. "Let me know if you think of anything else."

"Thanks. I will." After Hector drove away, Seth grabbed a rubber ball out of his truck and called Liverwurst. The dog bounded over to him, jumping in excitement as they went to the backyard. Seth threw the ball as far as he could. Liverwurst raced after it. The dog lived for playing fetch.

His cell phone rang, and he checked the screen. His former boss. "Hey, Chuck, what's going on?"

"I think I've got a dog for you. Remember Spud? Kendra trained him."

"I remember." The yellow Lab had shown a lot of promise with detecting fluctuating glucose levels.

"The placement fell through. The man had a stroke and has been sent to a long-term rehab center. If I could place Spud with another client, I would, but Kendra doesn't have time to train him. She's already booked out for months. I figure since you're the one asking, I'll go half price on the cost of the dog."

Spud. Happy, laid-back Spud. Seth had a soft spot for the dog. The thought of working with the Labrador excited him—he was a natural for diabetic alerts.

Seth's enthusiasm sputtered as he thought about who he'd be training it for—Caroline's daughter. Training a child meant training the parents, too. It equaled spending hours of time together, helping the dog learn the child's unique scents and how to alert adults to problems.

Could he do it? Spend weeks with Caroline and her daughter to get the dog up to speed? If it was for anyone but her, maybe.

"I appreciate the call," Seth said. "I'll talk to the girl's mother. Make sure she's crystal clear about what training this dog requires."

"You have good judgment, Seth. If you think this little girl can handle it, you have my blessing. You know the risks involved."

That he did. "If I begin training and I don't think Spud's in a good situation, I'll try my best to place him with someone else."

"That gives me peace of mind."

They caught up for a few minutes before ending the call. Liverwurst sat at his feet looking up at him with throw-the-ball eyes. Then the dog nudged the ball his way. He laughed. "Sorry, buddy. I got distracted. Good boy for being patient." He threw it again, and the dog raced away.

Thirty minutes later, with Liverwurst tired out, he headed back to the ranch, driving down Hickory Street, Fairwood's main drag. He passed brick storefronts, potted flowers, American flags, benches and lampposts. Then he turned onto the country road where the ranch was located and soaked in the sight of prairies and distant mountains.

Fairwood had always felt like home, even though it had never been his home until now. Every year as a kid he'd look forward to his summers here on the ranch with his grandparents, siblings and cousins. They'd help feed and check cattle—under Grandpa's supervision—eat hearty meals cooked by Grandma, play games, argue, run around and generally have the best times of their lives.

After graduating from high school, he'd returned for one more summer. Ken Bright had hired him to help take care of the herding dogs he bred. Ken had taught Seth how to train them—he specialized in Australian shepherds and border collies—and allowed him to help take care of the new puppy litters. Seth had thrived on their farm. He'd learned valuable skills and had known he wanted a career that involved dogs.

He and Caroline had been inseparable. He'd fallen hard for the farmer's daughter. But a week before summer ended, tragedy struck, changing the course of his life and hers.

Seth had no future with a woman who could think the worst about him.

Up ahead, the Hudson Ranch sign hung between two log posts. He drove down the long drive, past the lodge to the circular driveway where the cabins stood. After parking next to his cabin, he and Liverwurst strolled in the opposite direction to the lodge.

The big eat-in kitchen hummed with conversation. Brody was holding Jonah, his wife Lillian's nine-month-old baby—Brody and Lillian had gotten married in a small ceremony back in April—and Lillian and Meena were sitting at the oval table in the corner. Sonny stood in front of the range, stirring something that smelled delicious.

"How are you doing, Sonny?" Seth greeted him as Liverwurst trotted straight to Butch, the Bernese mountain dog who'd wandered to the ranch and claimed it as his home last winter. The dogs sniffed each other before plunking down on the hardwood near the window overlooking the backyard.

"I'm good. I hope you're hungry." The sixty-four-year-old had grown up on the ranch, and his father had been their grandfather's ranch manager for years. Last winter, Sonny had returned to Fairwood to live on the ranch and to bless them with his cooking skills.

"I'm always hungry."

"How did the meeting with the contractor go?" Hayden sneaked up behind him.

Startled, Seth clapped a hand over his heart. "I didn't see you there. When did you come in?"

"I was washing my hands. What's up with you? You're on edge."

He decided to ignore the comment. "The meeting went well. Hector's putting a bid together. If we approve it, he'll have his crew come in and start working as soon as we close on the property."

"That's good. Have you decided on a name for the center?"

"Not yet. Kylie's still sending suggestions." They wandered over to the table and found seats. "She's sent a few good ones."

"How many bad ones?" Hayden frowned.

"If I'm being honest, more bad than good. So far K-9 Kennels and Fairwood Pet Retreat are the only ones I can stomach."

"What were the other ones she came up with?"

"Ruff House Boarding, Dog Vacation and Bark Park Lark."

"Bark Park Lark?"

"Don't ask." He shook his head. "Not her best."

Brody handed Jonah to Lillian and leaned forward to address Seth. "Hey, I know this might be a sore subject, but I found out Caroline Bright moved back to Fairwood a few weeks ago. She's working over at Thompson Law."

Didn't he know it. Seth wasn't sure he wanted to get into this with them. They all knew what happened that summer. At the time, he'd explained everything to Hayden and asked him to tell the squad—too hard for him to talk about. And he hadn't mentioned her recent visit because…well, he'd hoped it would be the last time he spoke to her.

"Yeah, I know." Seth braced himself for questions.

"You do?" Brody's head jerked.

"After you guys drove away from touring the property last week, she pulled up in a minivan." Seth didn't know what to do with his hands, so he laid them flat on the table. "I guess she has a daughter. She asked for my help—"

"*Your* help?" Hayden interrupted. "She's got a lot of nerve expecting anything from you."

Privately, Seth agreed. "Her little girl has type 1 diabetes. She wants me to train a diabetic alert dog for her."

"Oh, that's so sad." Lillian had a soft heart, in part due to being bounced around foster homes as a kid and the recent death of her best friend, who happened to be Jonah's mom. "I can't imagine how worried I'd be if Jonah had diabetes."

Seth knew all too well how complicated life was as a diabetic. He'd placed dogs with several diabetics and had witnessed firsthand the difficulty of having to constantly monitor their glucose and either utilize an insulin pump or give themselves shots.

"I hope you told her no." Brody's expression was hard. "After the way she treated you."

"I told her I don't typically place service dogs with children."

"Good." Brody gave him a firm nod. "End of story."

"Not quite." He sighed, unsure how to make them understand. "I told her I'd make a few calls, and I did. I wasn't expecting anything to come of it, but Chuck contacted me today about a dog already trained to detect changes in glucose levels."

"Don't tell me you're going to let her have her way?" Brody's voice rose. Lillian covered his hand with hers, and Seth was thankful for her calming presence.

"I don't know, Brody." He shrugged. "I'll explain to her everything that's involved. If she thinks she and her daughter can handle it, I'll meet with the girl. But I won't waste a highly trained dog on a hyperactive kid who'll only confuse him."

"You're being very mature." Meena gave him an encouraging smile.

"I don't know about that." He could feel the heat rising in his neck. "I was pretty short with Caroline. I flat out told her we'll never be friends."

"Good," Hayden said.

"I'm going to give Kylie a call. Let her know what's going on." Seth excused himself and went to the living room, where a stone fireplace rose to the ceiling and a massive sectional couch surrounded a square coffee table. Accent chairs had been placed strategically around the space. He wandered to one of the side windows, pressed Kylie's number and stared at the prairie as he waited for her to pick up.

"Hey, did you like the names I sent you?" she asked.

"Two went on my short list. There's been a new development here."

"Oh?" Beeps from the nursing home came through.

"Did I catch you at a bad time? I thought your shift ended an hour ago."

"I'm walking out the door now. One of the CNAs called off and I had to cover until his replacement arrived. What's going on?"

He filled her in on Caroline, her daughter and the service dog, and his stomach knotted waiting for his sister to respond.

"That's tough, Seth." The car's engine roared to life. "Give me a sec. I need to switch to Bluetooth. There. Do you want to place Spud with her daughter?"

"I wouldn't mind working with Spud." The slow-moving cattle roaming the prairie had a calming effect on him. "But I don't want to work with a kid…or with Caroline."

"I don't blame you. How long would the training take?"

"Since Spud already knows how to detect changes in glucose, I think it should take a month—maybe two—to get him up to speed on the girl's scents and to teach Caroline and her daughter how to properly handle him."

"Sounds like you'd be spending a lot of time with Caroline." Her tone was thinner than tissue paper.

"Yeah." He didn't like it, either.

"Remember, she accused you of murdering her dog and puppies, Seth. Is that really someone you want to spend time with?"

"I don't *want* to spend time with her. I'd be teaching a dog how to detect her daughter's diabetes."

"Did she even apologize?"

"No. Not really." He'd cut her off before she could.

"Don't you think she should?"

Yes. He deserved an apology. But if she gave him one—a real one—his attitude toward her might soften. Then he'd be in danger of getting trapped in a no-win situation again.

"No. It would only complicate things."

"She burned you—like scorched earth—and I'm not sure this is smart. What if you become friends? Grow close?"

"We won't. Friendship is off the table. There will be no second chances."

"If you say so." The sound of the blinker mingled with her sigh. "I will admit, though, I think it's kind of you to consider helping her daughter."

The words he'd needed to hear. "You don't think I'd be making a mistake?"

A few moments passed. "No. I guess not. You'd be helping someone in need. Using your God-given skills. Plus, it will give you something to do while the center is being renovated."

That it would.

"Thanks, Kylie. I'll call Caroline. Maybe when she finds out exactly how demanding the next couple of months will be, she'll change her mind."

"Did you meet her daughter?"

"Not yet. And when I do, I'll say no if I don't think the girl is up to the task."

"Smart. I'll talk to you later."

Seth stared at the phone in his hand for a long time. Then he pulled up Caroline's contact information and called her.

He could only hope his instincts were spot-on. His family—including Kylie—was right. Caroline had hurt him once. He couldn't grow close to her, or he'd risk getting hurt again.

Friday night, Caroline sat in a booth at Taco Tony's and tried not to fidget. Seth would be here any minute to discuss the dog. She'd been surprised to get his call yesterday. Even more surprised that he'd asked her to meet him here to discuss what training the canine would entail. Her dad had agreed to babysit Nina, much to her daughter's delight, and Caroline had instructed her father over and over how important it was to keep his phone with him at all times and to call if Nina's reader alarm went off.

She'd showed Dad multiple times since moving back to Fairwood the insulin shots Nina might need and how to give them to her. She'd even created a graphic and laminated it with easy instructions. Just in case.

If her dad would get a smartphone, all this would be easier. Ken Bright was the most technologically challenged person she knew. Who had flip phones in this day and age? And forget texting. If it wasn't an actual call, he had no idea what to do. He wasn't even that old—early sixties—to be so averse to a smartphone.

Still, her dad loved Nina, and Nina loved him. He'd bred countless litters of dogs over the years and had good instincts when it came to the health of any living being. The fact that he adored her little girl meant everything to her.

But adoration and love wouldn't keep her baby alive.

The door opened, and Seth walked in. Her breath caught in her throat. Still gorgeous in his cowboy gear. His eyes narrowed, and he strode her way. Still hated her from the looks of it.

Couldn't say that she blamed him.

Caroline started to rise as he neared, but he waved for her to sit, then slid into the booth opposite her.

First things first. She needed to apologize. She'd needed to apologize for twelve long years.

"Seth, before we talk about the dog, I have to apologize."

He shook his head. "No need."

No need? Who did he think he was talking to? Of course there was a need.

"I'm sorry—deeply sorry—about all of the terrible things I said after my mom's funeral."

The pain in his brown eyes stabbed her conscience. "Apology accepted. We don't need to bring it up again."

It wasn't a suggestion. It was an order. She doubted the apology had gotten through.

"Seriously, Seth, I've beaten myself up so many times. I was wrong—"

"Got it. That's not why we're here."

Swallowing her disappointment, she stared at her ballet-pink nails. Every Sunday night she gave herself a manicure. Not because she was vain, but to maintain a professional appearance for her job. And to prevent herself from picking at her nails—a bad habit she'd worked hard to break.

"You mentioned a dog." She willed her mouth to curve in what she hoped passed for a smile. Showing him she had her emotions under control right now was as mandatory as the paint on her nails. She did what had to be done even when she was on the verge of falling apart. Story of her life.

"Yes." He visibly relaxed. At least a little. "It's a yellow Labrador already well trained to detect glucose levels."

"That's terrific." Hope bubbled up inside her.

"Not so fast." His warning glare popped a few of those bubbles. "He would need to be taught to specifically detect your daughter's levels. And the two of you would have to spend a lot of time working with him. Patience is key. He's a highly trained service dog, not a pet to ignore or goof around with."

The lecture, coming from him of all people, lit a fire in her core. She'd grown up raising puppies. Her father had taught her everything she'd needed to know about training dogs. She knew how to get them to listen and obey her. Who did he think he was talking to?

"I know how to handle dogs." She clenched her jaw. Could only imagine how prim and disapproving she looked, so she forced her mouth open a fraction.

"You don't know how to handle *this* dog." He leaned back, eyeing her with suspicion. "You'll need to be able to read his cues. You and your daughter—"

"Nina. Her name is Nina."

"You and *Nina* will have to be disciplined when it comes to him."

It was on the tip of her tongue to tell him she was the most disciplined person she'd ever met, but that sounded stupid. Besides, she needed his help. It wouldn't do to get snippy and ruin everything.

"Understood."

"You have to accept that the dog will be with Nina most of the time. Sleeping in her room, accompanying her to school in the fall—"

"The school's been adamant that only a certified service dog will be allowed to come with her to school." She wanted to pick at her fingernails so badly, but she refrained.

"Nina is insulin dependent, and according to the Americans with Disabilities Act, that qualifies her to have a service dog. I've been certifying canines for over a decade. This one *will* be allowed to attend school with her."

She didn't mean to exhale so loudly. But her relief made her shoulders drop as she tipped her chin up to stare at the ceiling. *Thank You, Lord.*

She'd worried that even if she found a dog for her daughter, she wouldn't be able to fully utilize it by having it accompany Nina to school. Seth had taken a large concern off her mind.

"You're absolutely certain the dog will qualify?" She had to make sure there weren't any hidden traps she'd missed about the whole school thing.

"I'm certain."

The man in front of her exuded quiet confidence. Younger Seth had been honest and dependable, but grown-up Seth was a man to be reckoned with.

And she found that very, very attractive.

Averting her gaze, she tried to compose herself. "Okay, so what do I have to do?"

As Seth explained the process—he'd be swabbing Nina's saliva at different glucose levels, teaching her commands to handle the dog, and the three of them would be spending hours with the dog to make sure he was properly alerting them—Caroline's nerves began to spiral.

She hadn't realized she'd have to spend so much time with Seth. All those summers ago, she'd fancied herself in love with him. Maybe she had been. Or maybe it had been a teenage crush. Either way, she'd ruined their relationship. And since then, she'd ruined every subsequent romantic relationship.

She had too many checklists. Needed to double-, triple- and quadruple-check everything. Her micromanaging personality had chased away the few men who'd tried to get close to her.

Basically, she was a control freak, and she couldn't seem to change. Nor did she want to.

"I'm not agreeing to anything until I meet Nina." He crossed his arms over his chest.

She blinked. Hadn't expected that hiccup. She'd thought this meeting was it—that he'd given her the green light for training the dog. "Why?"

"Because I have to make sure she can handle this responsibility."

"She can handle it."

"I'll be the judge of that."

The glint in his eyes brought her back to the worst day of her life. The day of her mother's funeral. She'd been numb from the shock of losing her mom in a car accident. Seth had offered to come over and take care of the new litter of puppies the morning of the funeral. Later, when the funeral was over, she'd slipped away to the barn where they'd temporarily moved Lucy and her puppies. Caroline had been desperate for some privacy, to give in to the tears that had refused to come out. She'd wanted to be with her favorite dog, Lucy.

And she'd been met with horror. The pen had been a crime

scene. Tufts of fur remained where the puppies should have been, and a trail of blood had led her to Lucy's body. The Australian shepherd and her pups had been killed by a predator.

She remembered Seth had just arrived. She could still hear her unnatural wail as he'd sprinted to her. Could still feel his hands clutching her biceps as he'd demanded to know what was wrong. She'd pointed to the dead dog, twisted out of his grasp and screamed, *"You did this! You were supposed to keep them safe. They're all dead! Because of you!"*

Family and friends had rushed outside at her scream. They'd heard every word she'd shouted. Seth had tried to ask her questions, but she'd physically pushed him away. Yelled that she never wanted to see him again. She'd never forget the expression—the betrayal—on his face. The hurt in his eyes. How pale he'd become.

She'd driven him away.

And she'd been wrong. Two days later, their neighbor's ten-year-old son had confessed to sneaking over to play with the puppies. He'd forgotten to latch the pen and hadn't thought to shut the barn door.

By then Seth had left town, and Caroline had been too devastated to make things right. With time, she'd found a new normal—without her mother, without Seth, without her favorite dog. She'd moved away, found a job. Grown up.

The sunshine in her life had departed…until Nina came along.

The noisy restaurant brought her back to reality.

"When do you want to meet her?" She raised her chin.

"Let's not drag this out. Are you free after church on Sunday?"

"I am."

"I'll come to your place." Then he got up and left without saying another word.

Strangely out of breath, she sank into the booth. So what if being around Seth again made her uncomfortable? Reminded her of her flaws? Drilled home the truth that no matter how hard she tried, she couldn't seem to stop herself from pushing away men she found attractive?

Success in life boiled down to one thing—protecting her daughter. Nothing else mattered. Not even Seth Hudson.

He had a lot of research to do before he could open the dog-boarding center—if he could just focus enough to do it.

The following morning, Seth perched on a stool at the counter of his cabin's kitchenette and sipped a steaming mug of coffee. His laptop screen faced him, and a notebook and pen sat next to it. All of his thoughts kept detouring to Caroline.

Why had she decided to apologize last night—at Taco Tony's, of all places? He had *not* wanted to hear it. And watching her cling to her composure when he knew her well enough—even after all these years—to sense she'd been itching to chip away at her nail polish, to argue with him, to get up and pace, had lowered his defenses.

Maybe that was what was getting to him.

She'd matured. Found a way to keep it together. But at what cost?

Who cared? Wasn't his concern.

He typed liability insurance and skimmed the results. Clicked on the most relevant one.

He hadn't been there when she'd found out her mom died. When she'd called him, he'd driven out to their farm as fast as he could. He'd held her, surprised she didn't cry. She'd seemed more stunned than anything. And two days later, she'd put on a brave face to stand beside her father at the funeral, greeting people and accepting their condolences.

Seth had taken care of the puppies—only six days old—and lavished extra attention on sweet Lucy while the Brights did their duties. Seth could still remember checking on the pups the morning of the funeral. Fighting his own sorrow, he'd held each one and kissed the tops of their little heads. Caroline's mom had been kind to him. He'd been upset about her death, too.

Later, when Caroline screamed at him near the barn, he'd been confused. She'd practically called him a dog murderer. Then he'd seen poor Lucy's body. Seth had thought it was his fault. Had he forgotten to close the pen? Had he somehow missed latching the barn door?

Ken never locked the barn during the day, so Seth hadn't even considered locking it. They always simply shut the doors and put the metal latch in place.

How many times he'd mentally reviewed the events of that day, he'd never know. Without evidence, he'd shouldered the blame. Figured it must have been his fault. Then, a few days later, Ken had called to tell him what had really happened. He'd determined a pack of coyotes had attacked Lucy and the pups. The careless young neighbor boy had been heartbroken and guilt-ridden.

Seth had hoped Caroline would call. That she'd apologize. Days went by. Weeks. And she never did.

He lurched off the stool and raked his fingers through his hair. Twelve years had passed. Shouldn't he be over it by now?

Her accusations still stung. All of the disapproving eyes on him as he'd gotten in his car still bothered him. They'd all thought he was responsible for allowing the puppies and Lucy to be killed. At the time, he'd taken the blame. He'd been more than willing to believe he was responsible for their deaths.

But it hadn't been his fault.

And Caroline had known it—and refused to apologize to him.

He drifted over to the front window where Liverwurst had curled up on one of the dog beds. Then he gazed out at the cabins opposite his on the circle drive and remembered a more recent betrayal.

He'd dated Samantha for six months. At first, she'd been understanding of his busy schedule. He'd warned her he traveled all over the country to work with clients and their new service dogs. But as time passed, she'd grown suspicious. He wished he'd been better at picking up on the clues. Maybe he could have prevented the meltdown of their relationship.

Samantha had accused him of cheating on her—with no proof beyond the fact she thought his nonstop traveling was "shady." She'd jabbed a finger into his chest. *"I'm on to you. For all I know, you have girlfriends all over the country."*

A relationship couldn't recover from that.

Accused of murdering dogs.

Accused of being a cheater.

What was it about him that women couldn't bring themselves to trust?

Seth shook his head and returned to the stool at the counter. Typed in another search. Jotted a few notes.

He had nothing against getting married. Having kids. But not if the woman didn't trust him. Not if she couldn't bring herself to give him the benefit of the doubt.

If a woman couldn't believe the best of him, he didn't want her.

He'd remain single and alone, thank you. He'd take the blind faith of a dog over a woman's accusations any day. Besides, he had enough on his mind at the moment. He couldn't get off course, not with so many things to get done before he could open the center.

Caroline's big brown eyes and her beautiful smile were a distraction. Nothing more. And he intended to keep it that way.

Chapter Three

"Remember, I need you to be on your best behavior. Mr. Hudson might have a special dog for you, but only if he thinks you can handle it."

Caroline straightened Nina's shirt and checked the time. They'd attended the early service at church, and Nina wouldn't need an insulin shot for another hour. Caroline did her best to feed her a constant carbohydrate plan. It made figuring out how much insulin to give her before each meal easier. Since Seth would be arriving any minute, she set an alarm on her phone to remind her about the shot. It wouldn't do to lose track of time and have Nina suffer for it.

How long would he stay? She couldn't imagine him needing an entire hour to determine if Nina was mature enough for the dog.

"I can handle a doggy, Mommy." Nina had changed into purple leggings and a long-sleeved T-shirt with a cartoon pony on it. Her long, dark brown spiral curls framed hazel eyes, thick eyebrows and a button nose. She carried a picture book over to the plush couch, climbed up and opened to the first page.

Nina didn't know how to read, but she'd memorized a few books. Sometimes she told the stories to her favorite stuffed animals. It would be nice for the child to have a sibling to play with, but Caroline didn't see that happening. Not with her track record in dating. She tried not to feel guilty about it, but that was easier said than done.

"Do you want me to put your hair in a ponytail?" Caroline studied the living room. Clean. No clutter. She'd dusted every surface and vacuumed the worn tan carpet last night. The sixty-year-old rental house might not be big, but it was in town and had a fenced-in backyard for Nina to play in. Caroline didn't mind that it hadn't been updated. The built-ins and old cabinets had a certain charm to them.

"No ponytail." She flipped a page, not looking up.

"Do you feel okay?"

"I'm fine." Her skinny legs stuck out straight in front of her.

"Tell me if you start to feel yucky." She looked out the front window at the empty driveway. He'd be here any minute. Were her insides being corroded with battery acid? She shouldn't be this nervous. "Do you have your reader?"

"Yes, Mommy."

Caroline narrowed her eyes at Nina's resigned tone. She'd been hearing it more and more lately. They'd only been living in Fairwood for three weeks. Maybe her daughter was struggling to adjust to a new town, new friends and a new daycare center. She crossed over to sit next to her. "I'm only asking to make sure you're safe."

"I'm safe." Another page flipped.

"You think you are, but we have to be careful."

"It's right here." Nina let out an exasperated sigh, patting her side where the clip-on case held the reader. Nina had only forgotten to clip it to her waistband a few times. The setup wasn't ideal, though, mainly because it was clunky for her tiny frame. Caroline had been considering buying a small elastic waist pack to keep it in instead. Another thing to add to her list.

"I want you to be very respectful and answer all of Mr. Hudson's questions as best as you can. No goofing around."

"I know, I know. You told me. I want to read my book." Her

little voice quavered at the end. Caroline went over to the window again. Was she being too hard on her?

A knock on the door set her feet in motion. She opened it, and Seth seemed taller standing mere inches from her than he had in the restaurant. He held a leash, and a medium-size dog resembling a tall beagle stood next to him.

"Hi. Come in. Thank you." Flustered, she opened the door wide for him to enter. "Have a seat. This is my daughter, Nina. Nina, this is Mr. Hudson."

Seth headed to the couch with his arm outstretched. "Good to meet you, Nina."

Standing near the couch, Nina, wide-eyed, clutched the closed book to her chest and tentatively shook his hand, not saying a word. Tension throbbed in Caroline's temples. Would he think the girl rude? Maybe she should have prepared her better.

"I like your dog," Nina said quietly.

"This is Liverwurst." He looked down at the dog. "If you'd like to pet him, hold out your fist so he can smell you."

Nina moved her fist toward the dog's nose. Liverwurst sniffed her hand and stared up at her in approval.

"He likes you. Go ahead and pet him if you want." Seth had gotten down on one knee on the other side of the dog.

"He's soft." Nina ran her hand tentatively across his back, then she giggled. "I like his floppy ears and pointy tail."

"I do, too."

"Is this the doggy that might be mine?" Her big eyes gleamed as she stared at Seth, and Caroline almost winced at the hope in them. *Please let Seth agree to this.*

"No, this is my dog."

"Oh." Her face fell. "I like him."

"I do, too." He pushed himself to standing. "You like dogs, huh?"

"Yeah."

He pointed to the couch. "Let's sit."

Caroline wasn't sure how Nina would react. With the exception of Caroline's dad, she wasn't around adult men on a regular basis. But Nina took a seat on the other side of the couch as Liverwurst settled on the floor next to Seth's feet.

"Liversmurf can sit next to me." She patted the couch cushion.

Oh, no. Caroline opened her mouth to correct her, but Seth chuckled and shook his head.

"He has to sit on the floor. And his name is Liverwurst. It's kind of hard to pronounce."

"Liver. Worse." Nina frowned. "Why does he have to be on the floor?"

"I don't allow him on the furniture. I've trained him to obey me."

"But it's not comfy on the floor."

"He doesn't mind. He has a soft bed to sleep on when he's at home."

"I have a soft bed, too. Want to see it?" She gave a little bounce of excitement.

"Nina," Caroline warned. The child flashed her an annoyed glare. Caroline kept her mouth shut and took a seat in a nearby chair.

Seth shifted to address both her and Nina. "If I brought a dog over for you, it would be a special dog."

"Special?" Nina asked.

"Yes. He's kind of like a superhero. He can tell when your blood sugar is too high or too low."

"Like my sensor does?" Her hand instinctively went to her upper arm where the sensor was installed.

"Yes, but this dog doesn't check your blood, he uses his nose. He can smell changes in your glucose levels."

"Really?" Nina's face screwed up in confusion. "I can't."

Seth's affectionate expression burrowed into Caroline's heart. How many times had that exact look been directed to her when they were teenagers? Too many to count.

"I can't, either," he said. "But first we'd need to spend time together to train him to recognize your scent. And I would show you and your mother how to take care of the dog."

Nina clapped her hands, her eyes shining bright. "I want a dog! I'll take care of him."

Was she being too eager? Too excited? Caroline picked at one of her fingernails, then forced herself to stop.

"It's a lot of work," Seth warned her. "You'll need to be very patient with him, and you can never ignore him if he's licking you or trying to get your attention. He'll need to sleep in your room and wear a special vest to go places with you."

"Like a superhero cape?" She clasped her hands together.

"Something like that. It wouldn't have a cape, though. Just a vest."

Caroline relaxed slightly. Seth was patient with Nina, and the girl hadn't done anything she considered a deal-breaker.

"Let's go outside with Liverwurst for a little bit." He stood and caught Caroline's eyes, asking the silent question if it would be okay. She nodded, feeling unsettled all over again. She wanted to warn Nina once more to be on her best behavior, but the girl had already hopped down and was on her way to the kitchen, where the door to their backyard was located.

Caroline caught up to Seth. "She's excited. She's never had a dog, and she loves animals."

The warmth he'd displayed with Nina vanished. "I need to see how she acts with my dog."

She wanted to tick off all the reasons Nina could be trusted, but from his icy demeanor toward her, she doubted it would sway him.

"This way." To her dismay, Nina had already gone outside, leaving the door open.

Caroline hurried outdoors. "Nina, you're supposed to wait for me. And you left the door wide-open."

"But Mr. Hudson said we had to go outside." She didn't sound rude, just matter-of-fact.

"Yes, but that doesn't mean you just run out there. You always wait for me, right?"

Chastised, she bowed her head. Seth and the dog went down the porch to the lawn, and the girl instantly perked up. Caroline bit back the rest of her lecture. Not the time or place.

"I'm going to let him off his leash." Seth unhooked it from the collar. The dog ambled to Nina, and she clapped again, jumping in delight. She looked two seconds away from throwing her arms around the dog and showering him with kisses. Somehow, Caroline didn't think Seth would be impressed if she did.

Her hopes began to evaporate like dew under the morning sun, but to her surprise, Nina showed remarkable restraint. She even held her hand out for the dog to smell her again, and then she stared up at Seth. "What do I do?"

"What do you want to do?" He cocked his head to the side, as kind as could be.

"I want to give him a hug, but he might not like that. Can I play with him?"

"Sure. Throw this ball, and he'll bring it back to you." Seth took an orange rubber ball from his pocket and handed it to Nina. She threw the ball toward the corner of the yard, but it didn't go far. Liverwurst ran after it and brought it back, dropping it in front of her.

"You did it!" She flung her arms around the dog's neck and kissed his ear. "Good job." Then she picked up the ball and dropped it with a grimace. "It's all slobbery! Yucky!"

Caroline closed her eyes. Seth wouldn't agree to train a dog for a girl who couldn't handle dog saliva. Plus, her hugging Liverwurst was probably a no-no.

If she could convince him that Nina wasn't always like this, that the child was simply excited…

Nina crouched and picked up the ball again, then she threw it and the dog ran after it. Her face flushed in happiness. They played a few more minutes, then Nina stopped throwing the ball. The reader began beeping.

Caroline's gut clenched as she hurried to Nina to check the numbers.

"Another shot?" Nina's face was noticeably pale.

"Nope. Juice." Caroline gently ran her hand over the girl's curls. "Be right back."

As she jogged up the steps of the back porch, she debated how much orange juice to give her, since she'd be giving her a shot of insulin soon. She figured four ounces should be enough to bring up her glucose levels.

She poured the juice and rushed back outside. Seth was sitting on one of the porch steps with Nina next to him and his arm around her. The alarm continued to beep. Sometimes the beeping got on Caroline's nerves. A constant reminder that her baby would never be able to live like other kids. Always tethered to sensors and insulin shots and counting carbs. It wasn't fair. But then, when was life fair?

"Here you go, baby." She handed Nina the plastic cup, and the girl drank it down quickly. "Let's go inside. You can watch a cartoon while Mr. Hudson and I have a chat in the kitchen."

Nina, still a bit pale and lethargic, nodded. "Can Liverwurst sit with me?"

Caroline looked at Seth.

"If you sit on the floor, then yes."

"I'll get my blankie and a pillow!" The juice was clearly kicking in.

"Nina, wait." She reached for her hand. "I'll help. Take it slow. Let your body adjust."

Nina slipped her small hand in hers, and they went up the remaining steps to the kitchen. Seth and the dog followed.

"Help yourself to something to drink," Caroline said. "I'll be right back."

She hoped the past half hour hadn't turned him off completely to the idea of training a dog for Nina. But what if he *did* agree?

She'd have to get on board with spending a lot of time around the man who was all smiles for her daughter and steely glares for her. Seth brought out her insecurities. Her nerves couldn't take his disapproval for long. Her nails probably couldn't, either.

He'd said they'd never be friends. And she believed him.

Something told her she'd be going through a lot of nail polish.

This wasn't going as planned. He hadn't expected to *want* to train a dog for Nina.

Seth sat at the small table in Caroline's tidy kitchen. The girl was young, yes, and excitable, but she was also aware of her situation and seemed willing to listen. He'd wanted to laugh at her disgust when she'd picked up the slobber-covered ball, and she'd surprised him by overcoming the grossness to throw it to Liverwurst again and again.

When her glucose dipped, he'd found himself wanting to protect her. And when she'd sat next to him on the steps while Caroline got her the juice, it had hit him how small and vulnerable she was. A teeny little thing. With a disease that could kill her if not managed properly.

He wished she didn't have diabetes. Seemed unfair—more than unfair—for a five-year-old to have to deal with that for the rest of her life.

Caroline's face appeared in the archway. "Give me one more minute."

"I'll bring over Liverwurst." He rose, signaling for the dog to follow.

In the living room, Nina sat on a child-size plush chair with a blanket over her lap. "Liverwurst! Come sit by me." She patted the carpet next to her, and Seth waited for the dog to get settled while Caroline found a cartoon on the television.

"You have your reader?"

"Yes, Mommy." No excitement in those words. Her flat tone pinched his heart. Must be tough for the kid to be reminded of her health problems all the time.

Soon he and Caroline sat across from each other at the kitchen table. He could tell by her steely posture she was on alert for Nina. An unexpected wave of sympathy came over him. Caroline might not deserve his sympathy, but he couldn't help feeling bad for her.

"Has to be difficult for you," he said.

She met his gaze. "Yes."

"She's a cute kid. Has your smile." Why had that come out of his mouth? He didn't want Caroline thinking he'd noticed her smile at all. He was here to evaluate Nina's readiness at being able to handle a service dog. That was all.

The way her expression shifted—eyes averted, mouth pinched—made him think she didn't want to hear him complimenting her, either.

"What's your verdict?" Was she clenching her jaw? This home visit had been wreaking havoc on his nerves, but he hadn't realized she hated the idea of being around him as much as he loathed the idea of being around her.

That alone should force him to decline training the dog.

Music from the cartoon reached him, as did Nina telling Liverwurst she thought the cat was funny.

All his excuses slid away.

He wouldn't deny Nina a diabetic alert dog. In his experience, these dogs were life-changers. They could alert their owners to problems before glucose monitors detected any changes. Didn't the girl deserve that?

Seth took a long look at Caroline. Shadows under her eyes. Worried expression. Eyes flitting around like she didn't know what to focus on.

Dare he admit the dog would help her, too? She'd be able to

sleep again. She'd have some peace knowing a trained canine was guarding her child.

"I think Nina will be able to handle the dog," he said.

Her sharp intake of breath surprised him. He covertly studied her, noting the tears forming. Her face radiated joy and relief.

"Thank you." The words were barely a breath. Her brown eyes shined with gratitude. "Thank you so much. I don't deserve this kindness."

"I'm not doing it for you," he said gruffly, turning his attention to the table. Seeing her like this sparked something dormant within him. He remembered what it had been like to be understood by her. To be valued by her. "It's for Nina."

"Whatever your reasons—thank you."

"But you'll need to find different childcare arrangements. The dog will be alerting her caregiver, and I don't believe he'll be successful in a daycare environment."

"I see." Her face fell. He could practically reach out and touch the worry spiraling around her.

"If that's going to be a problem…"

"No." She shook her head. "I'll figure it out. I understand. Really."

"Training the dog is going to take time. This isn't an overnight thing."

"I know." She nodded. "I'll do whatever you say. Nina will, too."

This gratitude—this proximity to her—was messing with his head. He pushed his chair back a few inches.

"I'll call Chuck and pick up the dog in the next couple of days."

"I don't want to put you out. I didn't mean to disrupt your schedule."

"My schedule is open for the moment." Setting up the boarding center was his main focus, but the paperwork he'd been dealing with didn't take all day. "We'll also have to introduce

Spud to Nina. Make sure they're compatible. We can work out a schedule after that."

Her forehead wrinkled as she bit the corner of her bottom lip. "What if they aren't compatible?"

Did she worry about everything? Reminded him of Hayden.

"If they aren't, I won't be able to train him."

"How likely is that to happen?"

"Not very." He didn't recognize this side of her. She'd always been so confident—the type to make a list and check it twice. She'd never worried about her plans, because she'd had complete faith she'd achieve everything she set out to accomplish.

"How long do you think the process will take?" The worry lines in her forehead deepened.

"I don't know. It depends on how quickly the dog recognizes her different scents and how well you and Nina take to the training."

"Is there anything I should be doing between now and when he arrives?" She reached for a pad of paper and pen tucked inside a napkin holder against the wall.

Caroline and her lists. He almost shook his head and teased her, but they'd passed teasing a long time ago.

"No. I'll get everything from Chuck. His food, toys, bed, you name it."

She jotted down what he'd said and glanced up at him. "Seth, how much is this going to cost me? I need to start making arrangements for payment."

Cost her? She thought he was charging her?

With his chin high, he shook his head. "Nothing."

"Nothing? That can't be right. Service dogs cost thousands of dollars. I know. I've done the research. Don't try to tell me otherwise."

"This dog won't cost anything. I'm not charging you for training." Seth had been forming impressions since arriving—from the furnishings to the house itself. Caroline was a single mom, worked as a legal assistant and was renting a small, outdated home. Nothing about her lifestyle was extravagant. Everything appeared neat, clean and…old.

If he had to guess, he'd say she'd purchased the furniture used and carefully added up costs when grocery shopping. He doubted her budget could cover a fraction of Chuck's discounted price.

Seth would pay Chuck for the dog himself. His gift to Nina. The inheritance he'd gotten from his grandfather, along with saving most of his salary for the past ten years, gave him financial options not many people had.

Caroline seemed mesmerized by her hands tightly clasped on the table. "I'd feel better if I paid you."

"Caroline." He hadn't meant to say her name, but the anxiety she kept trying to hide stirred him. She blinked. "There's no charge."

She reached over and covered his hand with hers. "Thank you, Seth. Thank you."

He discreetly slid his hand away, uncomfortable being this close, this intimate with a woman who'd hurt him so badly.

"I told you I'm doing it for Nina." He clenched his jaw.

Her cheeks grew red. "I don't care who you're doing it for. I'm just thankful you're doing it at all. I'll always be grateful. If you need anything—"

"I don't." He raised his palm. "I don't need anything."

He'd never need anything from her.

He couldn't afford to need her or get close to her. This time he could prevent a disaster by focusing on Nina. And in a month or two? There wouldn't be a reason to spend time together. Problem solved. He just had to stay strong and not grow attached to the beautiful mom and her adorable little girl.

Chapter Four

Why hadn't Caroline called him back?

The following Saturday morning, Seth strode down the lane from his cabin to the lodge with Liverwurst and Spud on either side of him. He'd spent all day yesterday traveling to Dallas and back to pick up the dog. His lunch with Chuck to discuss Spud's strong suits had felt like old times. Funny how a few weeks of not working with his former boss could feel much longer.

He probably shouldn't have wasted twenty-four hours picking up Spud when he still had so many business items to address. But he'd enjoyed yesterday all the same.

Spud had traveled well. He and Liverwurst were practically best buds already. Seth had a good feeling about the dog bonding with Nina. He'd have a better feeling if Caroline would call him back to schedule a time for him to introduce them to the dog.

Chattering birds flew back and forth between the trees overhead. Another great day with sunshine warming the skin on his arms where his T-shirt ended. He'd have a farmer's tan before he knew it.

Spud wasn't the only new arrival to the ranch. Cooper had driven in late last night. The only squad member missing from their new life was Kylie.

Seth opened the side door, let the dogs in through the mudroom and perked up at the lively conversation coming from the kitchen. A buffet of scrambled eggs, sausages, French toast and fruit sat on the island. They'd told Sonny he didn't have to cook on weekends, but the man always whipped up breakfast for them no matter how many times they urged him to take the day off.

"Coop!" Seth strode straight to his cousin, who was standing in front of the coffee maker, and clapped him on the back. "You made it."

"Barely." His dark hair was rumpled, and he looked like he could use a good night's sleep. He rubbed his eyes and poured himself a cup of joe. After taking a sip, he sighed. "I'm beat."

Seth glanced over at Spud. He and Liverwurst were sniffing Butch and wagging tails. Good. The three of them were getting along.

"How was the trip?" He turned his attention back to Coop.

"Long." Cooper yawned, then took another drink of his coffee. "Uneventful."

"This must be the dog for Caroline's daughter." Meena stood and went to greet Spud. The dog wagged his tail, eating up the attention. She petted him and told him what a good boy he was. Seth took the opportunity to pile a plate high with food and brought it over to the table to sit next to Brody.

"Will the dog live with them right away?" Meena asked.

"No." A piece of bacon dangled between his finger and thumb. "He'll live with me until he passes his training."

"What does the training involve?" Meena poured herself another cup of coffee and sat across from him. Cooper was wolfing down scrambled eggs like he hadn't eaten in days.

"Scent recognition. I'm training Nina on basic commands, and I have to teach Caroline how to know when Spud's alerting her. They'll have to be disciplined about the fact Spud isn't a typical dog. They can't ignore him or let him disobey their commands. It's not going to be a free-for-all."

Brody glanced sideways at him. "A free-for-all? What do you mean? Is Caroline one of those free-spirit types?"

"Kylie and I met her once when Seth worked at their farm. She's definitely not the free-spirit type." Meena dabbed a spill on the table with her napkin. "But maybe she's changed."

"She hasn't changed." If anything, she'd grown even more responsible. He chewed a bite of bacon before continuing. "Spud needs to know where he sleeps and where to go to alert Caroline and what to expect when leaving the house."

Brody seemed to consider his words. "I didn't realize so much was involved, but it makes sense."

"I'm sure her daughter can't wait to get started." The mug dangled between Meena's hands.

Seth swirled a bite of French toast into syrup. He'd thought Caroline would have jumped at the chance to get started, too. But he hadn't heard from her, and it had been almost a day. He'd called her yesterday afternoon in Dallas before boarding the plane. When she didn't pick up, he'd left a voicemail telling her he had the dog and to call him back so he could introduce Spud to Nina.

Had she changed her mind?

Of course not. He needed to stop letting his nerves dictate his thoughts. It wasn't as if he wanted to hear her voice or anything. He simply wanted Spud to be paired with her daughter as quickly as possible. Get it over with. Then he could go back to pretending Caroline didn't exist.

"What's the plan for today, Coop?" Seth figured it was as good a time as any to change the subject.

"Before you answer that," Meena addressed Cooper, "tell me what you think of your cabin. Did I nail it or what?"

She'd taken it upon herself to systematically renovate all eight of the ranch's cabins, and she'd been personalizing each one. Seth had to admit she seemed to know exactly what his had needed, from the colors to the dog supplies.

"Love it." Cooper grinned and stabbed a sausage. "It makes me feel relaxed."

"Minimalist." She nodded. "I know you're not one for clutter."

"I like the colors, too."

"Great." She rubbed her hands together. "Now I have to start Kylie's."

Brody stood with his empty plate in hand. "What about yours?"

"What about mine?" She stood, too, and skirted the table.

"You haven't touched your place. Don't you want to renovate your own cabin?"

"Well, yeah. I figured I'd get the others done first." They put their dishes in the dishwasher.

"Hey, I'll see you guys later." Brody waved to them. He and Meena continued talking as they headed to the mudroom where the side door was located.

Seth and Cooper finished their breakfasts in silence. Then Seth leaned back and eyed his cousin.

"We got sidetracked. What did you say you're doing today?"

"Moving van arrives in an hour."

"You need help unloading?"

"No. The company I hired is taking care of all that. But I'll need help unpacking if you're up for it."

"I'm up for it." He pushed his chair back and stood. "Can't wait to see your collection of Pokémon cards again."

"Ha-ha." Cooper followed him to the sink. "I parted ways with those a long time ago."

"Oh? Like last year?" He'd always enjoyed teasing Coop.

"It's been at least five years." He waited for Seth to rinse the dishes.

"Have you thought about what you're going to do here in Fairwood?" They put away the remaining food, and Seth added detergent to the dishwasher and started it. Then he signaled for the dogs, and they all headed outside.

"I've thought a lot about it, but I don't have answers. I figure I'll go over the herd's nutrition with Brody and Hayden as a start. I always liked checking cattle with Grandpa. I guess I'll be an extra hand around here until I get it sorted out."

"Sounds good to me."

Seth inhaled the fresh air. How he loved this part of the country. "It's wild, don't you think? Moving here?"

"Yeah, it is." Cooper already looked less exhausted than he had inside. The hearty breakfast and clear Wyoming air must be working on him already.

Seth's cell phone rang, and he pulled it from his pocket and checked the caller. Caroline. His heart pounded.

"I've got to take this." He halted. "I'll stop by your cabin after the call."

"See ya." Cooper continued on, holding up a hand.

"Hello, this is Seth." What a dumb thing to say. She obviously knew she was calling him. Why did interacting with her make him so fidgety?

"Hi, Seth. It's Caroline." Her voice made his insides feel funny. Like they had when he'd been eighteen. "I got your message. Are you free right now? Nina and I would love to meet Spud."

Now? Yes, he was free, but a wave of impatience hit him. Did she think he'd drop everything to come over there? *Like you have so much going on.* He should be pleased she'd called him back. It's what he'd wanted. They could move forward with the training. But a part of him balked at making it easy for her.

"I'm busy today." Not entirely true. Helping Coop unpack wouldn't start for a few hours, and he doubted it would take long.

"Oh, I understand." Her tone softened. "Let me know a day and time that works for you."

His annoyance vanished. "How about tomorrow?"

"Could we wait until after lunch? That way Nina will be at her best."

"Sure." Her words reminded him why he was doing this. For Nina. "I'll bring him over tomorrow around one."

They ended the call, and he broke into a jog to catch up with the dogs. He wouldn't think about why he had a spring in his step or why his earlier nerves had mellowed. *Careful. She burned you once.*

Hanging out with Cooper would get his mind off Caroline. He still had countless things to set up before he could even think about opening the dog-boarding center.

If he stayed focus on his goals—train Spud and get everything in place to open the center later this summer—he wouldn't have time for these weird feelings toward Caroline. But something told him that would be easier said than done.

"When is my doggy coming, Mommy?"

Caroline wiped the crumbs off the table and went to the sink to rinse the dishcloth. Nina had been wound up with excitement since Caroline had explained on the way home from church that Mr. Hudson would be bringing the dog over today.

"He's not your dog yet, remember?" It pained her to say it. She didn't want to remind Nina it might not work out, but she couldn't bear to give the girl false hope, either. Better to be honest with her. *Yeah, like you're being so honest with her. She thinks you're her real mommy. You haven't told her the truth about being adopted.*

"He will be." Nina had a dreamy expression. She'd changed into stretchy shorts and a T-shirt with a cartoon ice cream cone on it. "My super dog."

Caroline's father's words from last night echoed. *Let her be a kid.* Dad had grilled burgers for them at his house outside town. She loved the view from his back patio—a wide-open view of the land.

A few years after her mom died, he'd declared the farm too big for him, sold it and moved. Gotten a job with the post office, too. He hung out with the same friends—some were much older than him, and others were his age—but he'd never remarried, and he'd never gotten another dog.

She'd always wondered if she'd been the one to ruin his love of breeding and training dogs. So much had fallen apart after her mother's funeral.

"I hear his truck!" Nina raced to the living room and peered out the window. "I see the doggy, Mommy!"

Caroline wiped her hands on a towel, girded her shoulders and plastered a pleasant expression on her face. God hadn't gotten them this far with a service dog to let her down now. But she'd been let down plenty in the past, so what did she know?

The childcare problem Seth had mentioned was an issue. She'd asked her coworkers if they knew of anyone available to babysit, but the only recommendation was a young mom who was uncomfortable caring for Nina if it involved giving her insulin shots.

A problem for another time.

She hustled to the front door and opened it as Seth and the yellow Lab reached the porch. Attraction for the cowboy flared.

"Come in." She stepped aside and closed the door after they entered.

"Hi, Nina," Seth said. "I've got the dog I was telling you about. Meet Spud."

The way Nina was lightly bouncing on her heels with her eyes shooting off fireworks, Caroline figured she'd launch herself at the dog in roughly two seconds.

"Remember how you greeted Liverwurst?" He crouched on one knee next to the dog while keeping a grip on the leash.

"Like this?" Nina shoved her fist near the dog's nose. He sniffed it and gave it a little lick. She giggled. "He likes me. See, Mommy? He already likes me! He's the best dog!"

She didn't know how to respond, so she smiled and nodded. "I see."

Seth rose. "Why don't you give me the tour?"

"The tour?" Caroline drew her eyebrows together. Was he evaluating her house or something?

"So I can assess the sleeping arrangements and how they'll work for Spud." He addressed Nina. "Can Spud see your room?"

"Yay! My room!" Nina raced to the hallway. Seth, Spud and Caroline followed to her room in the corner facing the backyard. Soon Seth, Nina and Spud were all crammed into the tidy space with its twin bed, small dresser, bookshelf and toy bin. Caroline hung back in the doorway. Spud sniffed around Nina, and the girl took the opportunity to introduce him to a few of her stuffed animals, while Seth observed them.

What was he thinking? What was he looking for? Was he seeing any red flags that would cause him to take the dog away?

When the stuffed animals had been introduced, Seth shifted his attention to Caroline. "Where's your room?"

"This way." Her heart started fluttering as she crossed the hall. With wheat-colored curtains and a matching bedspread, it wasn't frilly, but it suited her fine. At some point, she'd add some framed art, but at the moment, she had enough to deal with.

"Do you need to go in?" She hoped he didn't.

"No. Just getting an idea of proximity. Spud will need to know where to find you."

That made sense.

"Can I take him to the backyard like we did with Liverwurst?" Nina stood next to Spud, petting his back. The dog's tail wagged and his mouth was open in a smile. Caroline was halfway in love with the Lab already.

"Good idea." Seth pointed to the hall. "After you."

By the time they made it outside, Caroline could hold in her question no longer. Nina and Spud reached the grass, and she hung back with Seth. "Well?"

"I don't see any reason they won't be compatible. Your house is easy to navigate, and it shouldn't be difficult for him to find you if Nina's in trouble."

Relief surged through her. She hadn't realized how uptight she was about this visit until now.

"Thank you, Seth. You've taken a load off my mind."

"We should start training right away." He leaned his forearm against the porch rail, keeping an eye on Nina and Spud. "What time do you get off work tomorrow?"

"Five thirty. Then I have to pick up Nina and make dinner."

"Would seven work?"

Seven was typically the first time all day she had a chance to get off her feet and relax. But this was for Nina, and Seth was doing her an enormous favor. Her meager free time would have to wait.

"Sure. Seven it is."

"Great. I'll bring the supplies so we can start getting Spud used to Nina's scents at various glucose levels."

"When do you think he'll be able to move in?" She'd have to buy kibble and figure out how to live with a pet again. She'd missed having a dog. Spud seemed perfect for her and Nina.

"It depends on how quickly he picks up on her glucose changes. I'm guessing three to four weeks. Could be sooner. Could be later."

A matter of weeks. That gave her time.

"We never really discussed her father." Seth shifted to stare at her. "Does he have custody—weekends? Summers?"

Nina's father? So they were having *this* conversation. "No."

"What does he think of all this?"

"He doesn't."

"What do you mean?"

"It's a story for another day." She pointedly jerked her head in Nina's direction. "He's not in the picture if that's what you're asking."

A shadow passed over his face, and her insides hollowed out.

Most of the time, no one cared that she was a single mom. But Seth clearly did. He had questions she doubted she'd be able to answer anytime soon.

But didn't she owe him something? For the dog? For helping her daughter?

Maybe. But she didn't owe him that. She didn't owe anyone answers she didn't want to give. Not even Seth.

Chapter Five

"Are you ready to get started?" Seth couldn't help but smile at Nina's eager face the next night. Caroline looked slightly less eager. Fatigue lined her eyes, but she had an air of enthusiasm he appreciated. Had to be hard on her working all day and coming home to make dinner and train the dog.

"Yes!" Nina jumped up and down, clapping her hands. Then she came up to Spud and began petting his head. "Hi, Spud. How are you today, puppy?"

The dog's happy expression and wagging tail boded well. He clearly liked the girl.

"What do you need from me?" Caroline arched her eyebrows, waiting for his response.

"Nothing." He unhooked the leash from Spud's collar, then unzipped the duffel bag he brought. "It will probably be easier to put everything on the table."

They went to the kitchen, where he began pulling out supplies—freezer bags, dental rolls, a Sharpie, dog treats and round training tins.

"What's all this?" Caroline leaned over his shoulder to inspect one of the tins. She drew her long brown hair to the side, giving Seth a view of the graceful line of her neck. Man, she was pretty. He averted his gaze.

"Training supplies." The quickening of his pulse needed to be stopped. He forced himself to think about her words from yesterday about Nina's dad not being in the picture. She'd acted like the guy didn't exist. The same as she'd done with Seth for twelve years.

She had no problem cutting men out of her life, and he'd better not forget it.

"I think Spud's thirsty." Nina and the dog came into the kitchen.

"I've got a bowl for him." Seth found the dog bowl in the duffel. Caroline took it, her fingers grazing his in the process. There went his pulse again.

"I'll fill this up." She pivoted toward the sink.

"What are those things?" Nina climbed onto a chair and sat on her knees, pointing to the dental cotton rolls.

"Cotton. For you to put in your cheeks when your blood sugar is either high or low." He handed her the package with the dental rolls. She flipped it over and handed it to him.

"My cheeks? How do I do that?"

Caroline set the bowl of water near the doormat and joined them. Spud's loud lapping made Nina giggle.

"Like this." Seth opened his mouth wide and pretended to put one inside his cheek. "Your saliva soaks into it. You have to keep it in there for a while."

"How long?" Her long eyelashes practically touched her eyebrows.

"About twenty or thirty seconds. Long enough for it to get good and soggy."

Her lips curved into a grimace, and he chuckled.

"Why do you need my spit?"

"Remember how I told you Spud can smell when your glucose changes? This is how we train him to detect your scents."

"Oh." She reached for one of the tins. "What's this thing? And why are there baggies?"

"Nina," Caroline warned. "Let's cool it with the questions. Mr. Hudson is helping us. Doing us a big favor. Remember?"

"It's okay," Seth assured her. "It's important for Nina to understand what we're doing and why we're doing it." The way the child beamed at him made him feel like he'd finished first place in a marathon. The only thing missing was a medal. "Spud has already been trained to detect high and low blood glucose levels for someone else. These cotton rolls and tins are for him to detect *your* levels. When he knows something's off, he can go get help. We're going to train him what to do when your glucose is in the danger zone."

"What's he going to do, Mr. Hudson?" She bounced in her seat, her eyes round as a Frisbee.

"First, he'll lick you and nudge you to make you aware you're not well. Then he'll go find your mother."

"What about when I go to daycare? Mommy won't be there."

Seth looked at Caroline, and she stepped forward. "We'll figure it out. For now, let's worry about training Spud." The smudges under her eyes reminded him again that she seemed tired. Had she been up in the night with Nina? Was she working too hard?

None of his business. He couldn't afford to start caring about her well-being.

"What's this for again?" The girl held up one of the flat, round tins. "Why are there holes in it? Is it a saltshaker?"

"No, it's not." Good. Nina could distract him from unwanted thoughts. "While you're at daycare and your mother's at work, I'll be working with Spud with these tins. I'll stick one of the cotton rolls with your saliva in it, then I'll hide it, and he'll get treats when he finds the tin."

"Hide-and-seek! Are we gonna do it now?" Nina opened one of the tins, her face dropping as she realized it was empty.

"No. Tonight you're going to learn a few commands for Spud. He already knows them, but it's up to you to use them correctly so he doesn't get confused."

"Oh, I like that." Her little shoulders lifted to her ears. "Mommy, we're going to tell Spud what to do."

"I'm sure you love the sound of that." Caroline's affectionate smile mesmerized him. He could stare at it all day. "What's first?"

He shook his head and collected his thoughts.

"Let's go to the backyard. It's too nice out to stay inside." Seth hooked his thumb toward the back door.

The three of them and the dog went down the porch steps to the lawn. Caroline crossed her arms to grip her elbows and yawned. Seth came over to her. "You can sit down and watch if you want."

"No, no," she said quickly. "I need to know what to do."

"You know the commands." He tried to be gentle with her. "You helped your dad do this countless times." The yard had no furniture, so he pointed to the porch steps. "Sit."

She hesitated, then nodded and sat on the second-to-bottom step.

"Are you ready, Nina?" he asked.

"Yes!"

He demonstrated the sit command. Then the stay command. He explained how she could have Spud lie down. Twenty minutes passed, and Seth noticed Nina's hands were trembling. Signs of low blood sugar. Spud zoomed to Nina's side and began wagging his tail and nudging her arm.

"He wants to play." Nina didn't have as much pep in her tone. "Do you have a ball?"

Seth immediately recognized the dog's alert. "No, Nina, Spud's alerting you."

"Why?" Her hand went to the CGM reader. "It's not beeping."

Caroline was by her side in a heartbeat. She checked the monitor and glanced up at Seth. "The reading is normal."

"Get some juice ready." He kept his voice calm and low, then turned to Nina. "Let's go inside. I'll carry you."

He scooped the girl in his arms and carried her up the steps. Spud glued himself to his side, and when they were in the kitchen, Seth set her at the table and praised the dog. Then he found the unscented soap he'd brought and washed his hands thoroughly. By the time he'd finished, the CGM began to beep.

"He knew." Caroline turned to him with wide, shocked eyes and a small glass of juice in her hand. "He knew before the monitor did."

Seth nodded, not wanting to miss this opportunity. He took two dental rolls and asked Nina to open her mouth. Then he slid them into each of her cheeks and turned back to Caroline.

"We have to get saliva samples now while her glucose is low. Then she can have the juice."

"Why can't I give her the juice first?" Her face twisted in worry. She pressed the reader to stop the beeping.

"It throws off the scent. Saliva samples can't be taken within thirty minutes of eating or drinking—unless it's water—or the dog will smell what she ate, not the changes in her glucose."

"That makes sense, but I don't like sitting here when she needs sugar. What if it gets too low?"

"Fifteen more seconds. That's it." Seth opened one of the freezer bags and counted the remaining seconds in his head. "Okay, Nina, you can't touch the cotton. Try to spit the rolls into this bag."

She nodded and worked one to the front of her mouth before spitting it in the bag. Then she got the other one out. Caroline shoved the juice in her hand and urged her to drink.

"Wait, Caroline, what does the reader say?"

"Sixty-two milligrams per deciliter."

As Nina drank the juice, Caroline exhaled loudly, clearly relieved. Seth rolled the baggie to get all the air out, sealed it and placed it in another bag. Then he labeled it with the date and the glucose reading.

"I didn't expect we'd get samples tonight." He studied Nina. She didn't seem lethargic, not like the episode when they'd first met.

"I didn't expect Spud would already know." Caroline shook her head in wonder and crouched down to the dog, scratching behind his ears. "Good boy. You're such a good dog."

Seeing Caroline petting Spud, hearing the special voice she used only with dogs, took Seth right back to being eighteen. He'd heard her use that voice every day with Lucy. Pain stabbed his heart.

Don't go back. Don't remember.

The dog's mangled body flashed in his mind, and he hated that poor Lucy had died so violently. Hated everything about that day.

"I don't think we can chalk it up to him smelling the change in glucose. Spud doesn't know Nina's scents yet. I think he picked up on her hands trembling."

"Well, whatever he picked up on, I'm grateful." Caroline beamed, giving the dog a final pat, and straightened.

"He still has a lot of work ahead of him." He didn't want her to get complacent or think the training wasn't necessary.

"I know."

Maybe he should give her more credit.

"Now that you've experienced Spud in action, I'll walk you through the steps to collect saliva samples when I'm not here. I'm going to need a lot of them." He was pretty sure his voice sounded normal, but he couldn't get this version of Caroline—the girl he remembered—out of his head. "Step one. Wash your hands really good with unscented soap. I brought some for you to keep."

As he described the steps, Caroline scribbled everything

down. By the time he'd finished, he was confident they'd be able to get samples on their own.

"We need more samples below seventy and above three hundred." He pointed to her notepad. "Jot that down."

"I would like to think her glucose won't be in those ranges." Caroline sounded wistful, but her expression grew melancholy.

"I would, too." Seth wanted to touch her arm, reassure her. "But this is Nina's reality, and we need to help Spud as much as we can for her sake. Now, I've taken up enough of your night. Spud and I are taking off. When can we come back?"

"Same time tomorrow?" Caroline handed him Spud's leash.

"Sounds good." He attached it to the dog's collar and grabbed the saliva samples and the duffel bag. "I'll see you two tomorrow night."

"'Bye, Spud!" Nina petted the dog one more time. "I love you!"

"I'll walk you out." Caroline accompanied him outside and waited for him to let Spud into the truck. "Thank you. I don't have the words to tell you how hopeful I am after seeing him in action."

"Like I said, he has a lot of work to do."

"I know." She nodded. "I'm just…grateful."

"Have you made any progress on the daycare situation?" He stood next to the driver's side door.

"No. I'm working on it."

"I just think the daycare will be too chaotic."

"I understand." She bowed her head. "I don't have many options."

He felt bad for her, but he had to stay firm. "A daycare full of toddlers and screaming babies will defeat the dog's purpose."

"I know. I'll find a babysitter."

"You've got time. He'll be with me until I'm confident Nina can handle him. I'll be giving him the Canine Good Citizen test before he can move in, too."

"You can do that?"

"I've done many."

"I appreciate all you're doing for me."

"Not for you. For Nina." He opened the door. "I'll see you tomorrow. Try to get some sleep."

As he drove home, his emotions bounced all over the place. He was proud that the dog had known what to do with Nina. Plus, Seth had already gotten saliva samples to work with. He could start working with Spud immediately. Tenderness filled him for the little girl who'd listened to his instructions. But her mother confused him. The woman had a heavy load to deal with and not much help from the looks of it.

Strange there wasn't a dad in the picture. No custody agreement. No answers to Seth's questions about him, either.

Caroline's ex wasn't his concern. He tightened his hold on the steering wheel. Whatever her life had looked like for the past twelve years wasn't any of his business. In fact, the less she told him, the better. He couldn't afford to get close to her again. This time there was a child involved. He'd rather saw off his arm than hurt Nina. He'd keep things polite and businesslike with Caroline. And protect himself in the process.eHe

"Grandpa, I can't wait to show you my super dog! He's soft and smooshy and smiles all the time."

"A super dog? The same dog you told me about on the phone?" Her father's teasing tone reminded Caroline of when she was a child. How she'd loved telling him all about her day back then.

"Yes! He's smart. I tell him to sit, and he sits. He's got big, happy eyes…"

As Nina continued to tell Ken all about Spud Friday night, Caroline stacked their dirty paper plates. They'd headed to her father's house after work, and he'd grilled fresh fish he'd caught himself. In the distance, green prairie grass waved like water in a river. The warm sun on her bare skin made her close her eyes for a brief moment. *Thank You, Lord.*

The weekend had finally arrived. The law firm had kept her busy all week, as did the training sessions with Spud every night. Seth had plans tonight, so they were resuming the training tomorrow. At first she'd been glad to have a night off, but she couldn't deny she missed him. She liked having Seth around.

"Be back in a second." Caroline took the stack of plates to the sliding door and paused. "Can I get you anything from the kitchen?"

"No, I'm full as a tick on a deer." Her dad patted his belly and laughed. Nina mimicked him by patting her tummy.

Inside, Caroline shoved the plates into the trash and washed her hands. Nina was getting better at using the commands Seth taught her. She'd had one high-glucose episode and two more low ones since Monday. Caroline had gotten saliva samples, but Nina had accidentally spit one of the dental rolls into a bowl of applesauce, and they'd both had a laugh at that. It had felt good to share a laugh with her daughter. Another thing she'd been thanking God for lately.

Laughter had been missing from her life for months. With Seth's help and the knowledge that Spud would be living with them soon, she was finally starting to feel hopeful instead of brittle. It had been a long year.

Her dad reached over and lightly yanked one of Nina's pigtails. Even through the glass door, Caroline could hear her yell, "Stop, Grandpa! That's my hair!"

He'd done the same to her many times as a child. He was a fantastic grandfather. And her mother would have been a terrific grandmother. She would have fussed and spoiled Nina. She wouldn't have cared Nina was adopted. It didn't bother her dad, either.

Caroline went back outside and took a seat. Nina was chasing after a butterfly.

"You doing okay?" Her dad eyed her.

"Yes. I'm better than I've been in a while. I'm so glad it's the weekend."

"You're working too hard."

"Nah." She waved in dismissal. "A little hard work never hurt anyone. That's what you always told me."

An affectionate smile lifted his lips. "How is Seth? I'm not surprised he ended up working with dogs. He always was a natural with them."

She swallowed the guilt his words brought up. "He's good. Very helpful."

"When the boarding center opens, I'll have to go over there and congratulate him." Her dad seemed pensive. But why?

"I'm sure he'd like that." She spoke the truth. Seth might be holding a grudge against her—for good reason—but she doubted he had an issue with her father.

"When does this *super* dog come and live with you?"

"I'm not sure. Seth's working with Spud to recognize Nina's blood sugar levels. Now that she has the basic commands down, we'll move on to teaching him what to do when he detects low or high glucose."

"Fascinating."

She suppressed a smile. Her dad was probably itching to ask Seth a million questions about training diabetic alert dogs.

"You should stop by. Seth's coming over tomorrow morning with Spud."

"I don't know."

"Why not?"

"Maybe another time. I always felt bad about how things ended between us."

And here she'd thought she was the only one with regrets.

"You called him. Explained. Had an adult conversation. I didn't."

"Yes, but..." He stared in Nina's direction, but Caroline

doubted he was watching her. She'd plunked down in the grass and was blowing on a puffy dandelion head. Her father seemed lost in his thoughts. She had a few questions of her own she'd never been willing to ask.

"Why'd you quit, Dad?" She tilted her head.

To his credit, he didn't ask what she was talking about.

"For a long time, everything reminded me of your mother." He gazed out at the horizon, where the sky showed streaks of pink. "The farm. The dogs. Everything."

She understood. "Any regrets?"

"Oh, I used to have plenty. If I wanted to dwell on the choices I made, I'm sure I could have done a lot of things differently. But no. No regrets. I wouldn't be who I am now if I had done things differently."

She wished she could say the same. All she did was push the past out of her mind, try to forget her mistakes. But they refused to be forgotten.

"What about you?" It was his turn to scrutinize her.

"Yeah. A few." She sighed. "I should have apologized to Seth back then. Before he drove away, or at least after we learned the truth."

"You cared a lot about him."

She had. She used to care so much about him. But she'd gotten over him. Hadn't she?

"I'm glad there's no bad blood between you," he said.

Was it true? Seth had been adamant they'd never be friends, but they'd worked well together all week. She wasn't sure how to define their relationship. "I wouldn't be too sure about that."

"Come on. He wouldn't be training this dog for Nina if he held a grudge." Dad settled deeper into the chair. "Nice having longer days, isn't it?"

"It sure is."

"What's happening at work?"

Thankful he'd changed the subject, she told him about the

call she'd gotten this morning from someone insisting the lawyer had misrepresented her, and Caroline had had to explain to the woman that she'd called the wrong law firm. The lady didn't even live in Wyoming. Her dad chuckled.

"Mommy, look." Nina ran to her with something cupped in her hands. Caroline leaned forward to see it. "I found a caterpillar. He's furry. Want to pet him?"

"Um, no thanks. I'll let you."

"I'd ask if I can keep him, but Spud's gonna live with us soon, and he might squish him." Nina turned away. "Come on, catty. I'll put you back."

"She's something, isn't she?" her dad said. "Best decision you ever made."

The backs of her eyes prickled. Why was she getting teary?

"When are you going to tell her?" he asked.

"Tell her what?" She knew exactly what he was talking about, but she didn't want to have this conversation again.

"You know." His gaze skewered her.

She began chipping at the polish on her thumbnail. "I'm not sure."

"Don't wait too long. She might be young, but she'll have questions soon."

"I know. I'm just dealing with a lot. I need to get through the summer. Have Spud move in. Then school will start—"

"Life isn't going to slow down anytime soon, Caroline. She'll be in sports, going to sleepovers, learning to drive. There will always be one more thing to get through."

Leave it to her dad to bring up the difficult things she'd been avoiding. Telling Nina she was adopted topped the list. "I'll do it when the time's right."

"The time might never be right."

Her neck muscles tightened, and she continued to chip away at the polish. Her dad brought up a valid point. But if she added one more problem to her already-teetering tower, it would topple over, and she wasn't sure she wouldn't completely fall apart if that happened.

When Seth had asked about Nina's father, she'd successfully punted the conversation. If he asked again, what would she tell him? And when Nina went to school, kids were bound to ask her about her family. They'd want to know about her daddy, and her daughter would have no answer.

Her dad was right. She needed to explain to Nina that she was adopted. But she couldn't handle it now. And until she could, she wasn't bringing it up.

A night with the guys. Exactly what Seth needed.

Friday night, he carried a stack of wood from the back of the UTV to the fire pit surrounded by rocks on a remote section of the ranch. Hayden and Brody had ridden horses to the area, while Seth and Cooper had taken the UTV. Liverwurst and Spud were in his cabin.

"Grab the cooler, will you?" Brody's commanding voice filled the air.

"Got it." Cooper grabbed the handles of the cooler they'd filled with soft drinks and water.

Seth dropped the wood on the ground while Hayden set up the camping chairs. The sky flamed hot pink and orange. Another half hour and daylight would be gone. He hoped the stars would be on full display. He loved sitting back and staring up at the constellations. God's creativity never ceased to amaze him.

Brody dropped a grocery bag full of snacks on the ground next to one of the chairs. "About time we had a guys' night. It's been way too long."

"Tell me about it." Seth elbowed Cooper out of the way to open the cooler. "Who wants something to drink?"

He tossed cans to each of them except Hayden, who was arranging logs in the fire pit. He lit a wad of newspaper. Flames shot in the air.

"You better fan those flames or the fire will go out." Brody held his can an arm's length away to open it. The soda bubbled over.

"I know what I'm doing." Hayden shot him a glare over his shoulder.

"The fire's not going to take." Brody reached for the piece of cardboard on the ground, but Hayden snatched it up first.

"I've got this. Do you really think I can't make a fire? I've been doing this longer than you have."

"That's stretching it." Brody rolled his eyes. "Grandpa always asked me to add logs."

"And he always had *me* start the fire." Hayden rose and faced Brody. The two of them had a silent standoff, then Brody punched Hayden's upper arm and grinned.

"Fine, man, get back to it." Brody turned to Seth and Cooper. "What's happening with the boarding center?"

Seth cringed. He'd been spending so much time working with Spud during the day and Nina and Caroline at night, he'd fallen behind on his list for the center.

"I'm working through paperwork." It was kind of true. He'd started filling out forms to submit to the state.

"Settle on a name yet?" Brody asked.

"Yep. Hudson K-9 Center. I was going to go with Hudson Kennels, but I think 'center' fits it better. That way people know I don't only offer boarding."

"Reflects the business better." Cooper raised his soda.

"I like it." Hayden, satisfied the fire wouldn't fizzle out, cracked open his drink. They all took seats in the camping chairs.

"Kylie came up with a winner," Seth said.

"Any progress getting her to move here?" Hayden took a sip.

"No." Seth leaned forward, resting his elbows on his knees. "I don't get it. She used to complain about her job all the time.

What's keeping her there? It's not like she can't get out of the lease for her apartment."

"I don't know." Brody shrugged. "Maybe the unknown. Every time we bring it up, she says the same thing—that she doesn't know what she's going to do here."

"Didn't stop me." Cooper relaxed into his chair. "I still don't have a clue what I'm doing with the rest of my life."

"Yeah, but you're already helping us with the herd's nutrition." Hayden fanned the fire again.

"Have you had any trouble accessing the herd-management software?" Brody asked. "I haven't spent much time on the nutrition side of things."

"That's because you knew I'd be moving here."

"True." Brody grinned. "You'll understand how to add the breakdown of the different grasses from the pastures and all that, right?"

"It's going to take some time to get everything analyzed," Cooper warned.

"We're not in a hurry, are we, Hayden?" Brody said.

"Nope. I'll leave the nutrition to you, little cuz." Hayden smirked at Cooper.

"Little?" Coop sounded offended. "Watch yourself. I'm two inches taller than you."

"A quarter inch, tops."

As they argued over who was taller, Seth shook his head. Some things never changed. The four of them had been doing this since they were kids.

"Knock it off, you two." Brody must have gotten sick of the bickering. "Seth, now that we closed on the property, did the lawyer contact you with the business paperwork to sign?"

"He did." Hudson Ranch Inc. used the same law firm their grandfather had used for years.

"Have you gotten bids on liability insurance?" Brody narrowed his eyes.

"Yes." He'd done that last weekend. "I downloaded the application for a local business permit on Thursday, and Hector said demo begins on Monday."

"Hey, did you have a chance to look over the dog-boarding software I sent you?" Cooper asked.

"Not yet." Another important task he'd ignored.

"Pay attention to the processing fees," Brody said.

"I will. That's why I haven't made a decision on what to purchase." Not technically true—he hadn't wanted to spend hours comparing services. Boring.

"If you want help, I'm into that sort of thing." Cooper gave him an encouraging nod.

"Thanks." Seth appreciated Cooper's analytical business mind. "I already planned on running it by you."

"I'm looking forward to it."

"Now—" Brody stared at them all to make sure he had their attention "—we all want to know what's happening with Caroline, the kid and the dog."

"Nothing's happening," he said, rapid-fire. "I'm working with Spud on scent recognition using Nina's samples. He's doing really well."

"How does that work again?" Hayden kept one eye on the fire as the sun dipped lower, and the sky grew dark.

"I hide a sample in a special tin. I time him to see how long it takes for him to locate it. When he alerts me, he gets a treat. He's fast. All the training he'd been through before I brought him here has really paid off."

"I'm glad to hear it," Brody said. "What's next?"

"I'll keep working with him on low and high glucose detection."

"And?" Brody dragged out the word.

"And what?" He didn't mean to sound curt.

"If you're working with him here, why are you going to Caroline's each night?" Hayden frowned.

"I'm training them how to handle him." His brother could be annoying. Hayden acted like Seth was going over there for friendly visits. He wasn't. Although he had to admit he looked forward to their sessions. Caroline was a good mom. Strict and loving. On the overprotective side. He'd probably be the same if he had a cute kid like Nina. As it was, he wanted to protect her, and he barely knew her. "I'm teaching Nina basic commands with Spud. Sit. Stay. Drop it. That sort of thing."

Cooper pulled a face. "Kids that age are like tornadoes. Hard to get them to sit still."

"She's smart. Listens to me. It helps that she loves Spud. They seem meant for each other."

The crackle of the fire filled the air as silence settled.

"If no one is going to ask it, I will," Hayden said loudly. "Are you getting close to Caroline?"

"No," Seth sputtered. "Come on. You know me better than that."

"Do I?" Hayden gave him the don't-lie-to-me-brother look. "She's not exactly ugly."

"No one would describe Caroline Bright as ugly." Brody narrowed his left eye and pointed to Seth. "I've been in town enough to hear the locals talking about her. They've all noticed she's a stunning woman."

Seth clenched his jaw. Great. The single guys were probably tripping over themselves to ask her out. Made him want to gag. Just because he didn't want her didn't mean he could stomach watching some other guy date her.

"Not my problem." He poked a long stick into the fire.

"If you need us to remind you what she did to you…" Brody let the words trail off.

"I don't need any reminders." He wanted to stand and pace, but the guys would make a big deal out of it. Accuse him of getting worked up. "I don't think of her like that."

Not technically true. Spending time with her had brought

back old feelings. He remembered all the reasons he'd been so smitten with her in the first place. She was a good listener, got things done and cared about her loved ones. Sure, she had some bad qualities, too. In his mind there was only one bad quality, and it was a doozy. If she could see the best in him, maybe they'd have a chance. But that was a big if.

"Can we talk about something else?" he asked. "Brody, have you and Lillian decided where to live?"

"The cabin fits us for now. We've talked about building a house, but we're just talking at this point." Brody began filling them in on what part of the ranch made sense for them to build, and Seth promptly tuned him out. He stared up at the sky, biding his time before the stars appeared. He'd gotten the guys off his back about Caroline for now, but it was only a matter of time before they brought it up again. And the next go-around, he might not be so adamant about denying his attraction.

He'd better remind himself why Caroline was off-limits. Or he'd never hear the end of it.

Chapter Six

The center's renovations were in full gear. Seth parked next to the pole barn and imagined the different dogs he'd be boarding here. He couldn't help but get excited. A little over two weeks had passed since the bonfire at the ranch. On Saturday, he'd joined the squad—even Kylie had been able to make it—to watch the Fourth of July fireworks. They'd all had a grand time. How long had it been since he'd enjoyed simple summer pleasures like watching fireworks? What else had he been missing? Rodeos. He hadn't been to one of those in years. He'd have to remedy that soon.

He got out of his truck with Liverwurst and Spud. They ambled next to him all the way into the barn.

Inside, power tools made it difficult to hear anything. Seth spotted Hector, who raised his hand and strode his way. Seth estimated half a dozen workers were busy installing the wiring and framing. And here he'd been worried the work would drag out for months. Dust filled the air, and piles of discarded supplies stood in mounds throughout the space.

"Let's go outside," Hector said. "Too loud in here."

Seth agreed, and the dogs led the way outdoors. The hot air settled like a wet blanket on him. Seth shifted his cowboy hat to wipe his forehead.

"Looks like you've already gotten a lot done." Seth looked back at the building.

"That's how we work—methodically and quickly. We did find more damage in the far corner. A rodent chewed through wires. Nothing major. And the plumber wants to replace the shower and toilet in the house. I told him you'd have to approve it."

"What's wrong with the shower and toilet?"

"They're old, and he needs to replace the subfloor. Water leak. Best to buy new."

Seth nodded. "Sounds like I'd better take care of it now or I'll be dealing with more water damage later."

"Exactly."

They spent the next twenty minutes going over the rest of the progress, then Hector went back into the pole barn, and Seth weighed his options. Drive back to the ranch or hang out here?

The dogs sat beside him, panting in the heat.

He had a third option.

He could stop by Caroline's. She'd told him she had the day off since the Fourth of July fell on a weekend this year. He wouldn't be going over there to hang out or anything. Just wanted to say hi. Maybe see if she and Nina would like to go to the park. Nina could practice walking Spud with a leash. And he could help her get used to being out in public with the dog.

Yes, a stop there made sense. To help Nina with Spud.

"Come on you two. Let's get out of here." After they were settled in the truck, he drove to Caroline's house, trying to ignore the topsy-turvy sensation in his stomach. He'd been getting along well with her. They spent every evening together for training, and his attitude had been softening. She was a caring mom. He admired that she was raising the girl with values. Caroline never complained, although he knew being a single mom to a child with health problems couldn't be easy. Her expectations were high, but he didn't hold that against her. She'd always been a perfectionist.

It didn't take long before he was knocking on her door.

Maybe he should have texted her first. What if she was busy? Or running errands? He didn't want this to be awkward.

The door opened, and Caroline's face broke into a smile. Her hair was pulled back into a high ponytail, making her look eighteen again. The little wrinkles at the corners of her eyes gave her age away, though, and he found himself liking grown-up Caroline even more than teenage Caroline. *Yikes.*

"I hope you don't mind me stopping by." He glanced down at the dogs. They remained seated, but Spud's tail was wagging. The dog loved coming here. Nina would be a good placement for him.

"Not at all." She wiped her palms down the sides of her shorts. "Come in."

As soon as Spud was inside, Caroline crouched to pet him. "How are you, boy? It's too hot out there, isn't it? Do you want water? Come on. You, too, Liverwurst." She motioned for the dogs to follow her to the kitchen, and they both lapped up the water from the bowl near the back door.

"Where's Nina?" Seth noted the citrus smell of cleaning products. "I was hoping the three of us could go to the park. It would give her a chance to practice handling Spud on his leash."

"She was in her room looking through a picture book and fell asleep. I should go check on her." The smile faded and worry crept in. "I'll be right back."

"Why don't you bring Spud? He's a pro at detecting the saliva samples. I work with him every day, and he finds them within seconds. He'll be able to detect if anything's off with her glucose."

"I will." She nodded, looking thoughtful, then gave him a smile. "Thanks."

While she headed down the hall, Seth petted Liverwurst, then gazed out at her backyard. She'd put a few chairs and a small table out there last week. Sure would be nice if Nina could have a play set, too, but he knew better than to bring it up. He didn't want to embarrass Caroline about finances. A trip to the park today would be good for them all.

"She's still asleep. Spud checked her out and walked away, so I think she's fine." Caroline's face flushed as she breezed past him to the refrigerator. "I'm thirsty. Do you want anything?"

"Whatever you're having."

A few minutes later, they sat across from each other at the kitchen table. "How is the center coming along?"

"Great. The place is a wreck—in a good way. They're finishing up the framing and starting to install the new wiring. I have to admit I'm having a hard time imagining the final result. I can't picture in my head what it will look like, even with Meena's digital renderings."

"It will be fresh and new and just right. The community doesn't know how good they're about to have it. You have a gift with dogs."

Memories of working with Caroline and her father to train dogs came to mind. He wanted to play a round of *remember when Toggle tried to herd a rooster and the bird chased him? That dog sprinted away with his tail tucked between his legs.* But that would invite more memories, would bring him closer to her, and they were close enough.

"How's your job going?" he asked. No warm, fuzzy feelings with that question.

"Good." She nodded, but her expression held no enthusiasm. "Busy. Mr. Thompson has been giving me more responsibilities. I'm organizing the case files for new clients."

"You're a natural at organizing." He didn't miss her slight frown. "What? Is there something wrong with being organized?"

"No." Her tight-lipped expression didn't set him at ease.

"Why'd you make that face? I'm confused."

"Nothing's wrong. I like my job. I *am* organized."

"Then what's the problem?"

"Not everyone sees my organizing skills as a positive thing."

"Your boss clearly does." As he should. Who wouldn't want an employee who was efficient and could easily find anything they needed?

She averted her eyes. "I've been accused of being a control freak. Not by my boss, though."

Understanding dawned. Maybe that was why Nina's dad wasn't in the picture.

"I never thought of you that way."

"You didn't?" An embarrassed laugh escaped. "I'm sure you're aware of my type-A personality."

"You get things done. It's a positive thing." Against his better judgment, he probed further. "Why does it bother you?"

"It doesn't bother me. Forget it. Let's drop it."

"Okay." He stared at the glass in front of him. A bead of water dripped down the side. Well, this was fun. Sitting here awkwardly with the woman he wasn't supposed to be friends with but couldn't help wanting to cheer up. Seconds ticked by.

"My ex-boyfriend didn't like that part of my personality." The words were crisp. "He was hoping for a more go-with-the-flow girlfriend, and he thought I fussed over Nina too much. To be fair, he had a point with the last part." Her self-deprecating smile didn't reach her eyes.

Indignation festered. The guy clearly hadn't understood what a blessing Caroline's personality was. And she was only trying to protect her daughter. Or was she that guy's daughter? He squirmed with the discomfort of wanting to ask, but needing to stay ignorant.

"Was the boyfriend—ex-boyfriend—her father?" There went staying ignorant.

"No." She sighed and looked back over her shoulder to check for Nina and leaned in. He leaned in, too. She lowered her voice. "This stays between me and you."

Seth nodded. Whatever she was about to tell him was clearly serious.

"I adopted her."

Caroline had adopted Nina? He sat back, stunned. "How?"

She looked back again and kept her voice barely above a whisper. "My former coworker Beth told me her cousin was coming to stay with her for a few weeks. I found out Beth was trying to counsel the girl. She'd just graduated from high school, and her boyfriend dumped her after he found out she was pregnant. The girl had college plans and felt hopeless."

Seth could picture the scenario easily.

"I didn't plan on getting involved, but I felt bad for her, and I asked Beth if I could take them out to dinner. The girl admitted she didn't want her stepmother or friends knowing she was pregnant. I asked her if she'd be willing to give up the baby for adoption. She didn't seem interested, and I didn't push her. The three of us spent time together over the next couple of weeks, and I couldn't bear to think of the baby not having a chance to live. But I wasn't married, and I wasn't ready to be a mom. It didn't occur to me to ask her to let me adopt the baby."

Of all the questions swirling in his mind, one thing he didn't question was Caroline's sincerity. Of course she couldn't bear to think of the child not having a chance to live. He'd witnessed her helping deliver puppies. She lavished attention on every living creature in her path.

"Two days before she was set to leave, the girl came to me and asked if I would adopt the baby. She said she could live with herself if she knew I raised it. I was shocked, but not shocked, you know? I tried to steer her to allow a married couple to adopt the child. But she wouldn't budge. It was me or ending the pregnancy. So I said yes. Beth talked to the girl's dad and stepmom, and they all agreed it would be best for her to stay with Beth until the baby was born. We had the paperwork drawn up for a private adoption. And she was able to start college during the winter semester."

"I take it Nina doesn't know."

Caroline shook her head. "I'll tell her when I'm ready. And the mother doesn't want her identity revealed."

"Nina deserves to know she's adopted." He kept his voice quiet.

"And she will." She began chipping polish off her index fingernail. "You sound like my dad." Her fake laugh didn't fool him. Keeping the secret bothered her.

"I give you credit, Caroline. Most people wouldn't have done what you did."

"I can't imagine life without Nina. She's the best thing that's ever happened to me."

He nodded, but her comment raised another question. What was the best thing that ever happened to him?

Training service dogs? Maybe. It used to fulfill him, but Seth couldn't claim it was the best thing to ever happen to him.

He was still waiting for his best thing.

"I'm still trying to find another childcare option. I don't want you to think I've forgotten."

"My cousin Meena seems to know everyone and everything in Fairwood. Want me to ask her if she knows anyone who babysits?"

"Would you?" Her big eyes glistened with hope. "I want Spud to live with us as soon as possible, and I know the daycare situation could hold it up. Plus, it would be helpful to have someone else to rely on for her care."

The things she wasn't saying became clear. "You never get a break, do you?"

A crease formed between her eyebrows. "From Nina's care? Yes. Eight hours every workday."

"And you worry about her the entire time, don't you?" He kept his tone light. Didn't want her to think he was judging her.

"Wouldn't you?" she snapped. Then she balled her hands into fists and placed them on her lap. "I do worry all day. But having the CGM and the app on my phone helps. I'm getting better. When Spud moves in, that will take a big load off my mind. She's just so…little." Her voice broke at the end, and her lost expression pushed away all the past hurts he'd been clinging to.

Seeing her like this—vulnerable, scared—made him want to wrap her in his arms and tell her she didn't need to worry. That he was right here. He wouldn't let anything happen to Nina.

But he couldn't. Because he had no plans to be part of her life. And even if he did, he couldn't prevent anything happening to Nina any more than she could.

"Mommy?" Nina appeared in the archway. Spud trailed behind her. She rubbed her eyes, then perked up when she spotted Seth. "Mr. Hudson!"

She raced to where he sat and beamed up at him.

"Hey there, Nina."

"Why are you here?"

"Your mom and I thought you might like to go to the park and walk Spud on the leash."

"Really?" She clearly loved the idea. "Yay! I get to hold the leash?"

"You sure do." His heart was dissolving into mush. First Caroline's honesty had worn down his resistance to being her friend, and now this cutie was acting like he was her hero for letting her walk Spud on a leash.

He never should have gotten involved with these two. But he was sure glad he did.

How long had it been since she'd simply relaxed at a park on a summer day? She couldn't remember. Caroline strolled next to Seth, and Nina walked on his other side as he explained how to hold Spud's leash and told her how the dog was supposed to behave. Caroline was holding Liverwurst's leash, and he walked loosely beside her. She'd forgotten how much she'd loved spending time with dogs. Her entire life had been filled with canines until her mom died.

"See how he's starting to get ahead of you?" Seth pointed to Spud. "Tell him to heel."

"Heel, Spud." Her high-pitched voice tugged at Caroline's heart. Five years old and growing up so fast. But she'd always be her baby.

She discreetly looked past Seth to check on Nina. Her cheeks were flushed. Was it too hot out? Maybe they should have stayed home. She didn't want Nina overdoing it and paying the price.

Good thing she'd brought a travel cup with ice water and had shoved a small, soft-shell travel cooler with Nina's supplies into the lightweight backpack she wore.

"Good," Seth said. "That's what he's supposed to do. Stay next to you. Not lunge ahead."

"But what if he sees a squirrel?" Nina asked. "He'll want to chase it."

"That's why you're training him to stay next to you. He's not allowed to chase after squirrels."

"What about a bear? He'd *have* to chase a bear, right?"

"No again. He's not allowed to chase anything while he's on duty."

"And his vest tells him he's on duty."

"Correct."

"I like that it's red. But I like pink, too. Could he have a pink vest?"

"He can have any color vest as long as it says 'Medical Alert Dog.'"

Caroline bit back a chuckle. Seth had so much patience with her daughter.

"I like his pocket, too," Nina said. "Do you think I could fit my Chapstick in there? Grandpa bought me strawberry kind."

"It's only for your information and your hard candies. He can make sure an adult helps you quickly."

"I don't like shots." The words came out matter-of-fact, but they bruised Caroline the same. She wished Nina didn't have to take insulin. If she could take them for her, she would.

"I wouldn't like them, either," Seth said. "You're brave. I cry like a baby when I have to have a shot."

"You do not!" Nina giggled. "Cowboys don't cry."

"Who said I'm a cowboy?"

Caroline glanced his way, noting the way his eyes creased in the corners. Who would have thought Seth Hudson would be teasing her sweet Nina? Not her.

"You wear a cowboy hat and boots." Nina's tone was all business.

"I do?"

"Yes, silly! See?" Nina halted and pointed at his boots, then at his hat.

Seth stopped and took off his straw hat. He pretended to study it, and then set it back on his head. "I guess I *am* wearing a cowboy hat and boots. If I'm a cowboy, I can't cry when I get a shot, can I?"

"Nope."

"I might need you to hold my hand."

She giggled with glee.

Caroline wasn't sure what to make of his teasing and Nina's enjoyment of it all. She enjoyed it, too. Who wouldn't? But what would happen when Seth wasn't part of their lives anymore? He'd been quite clear they'd never be friends. Poor Nina would miss him.

And Caroline would, too.

"The playground!" Nina poked her head around Seth to address Caroline. "Can I play, Mommy?"

"I don't know. It's awfully hot out." The words were out before she had a moment to consider.

"I'm not hot." Nina shook her head, but her pink cheeks said otherwise.

"Here, have a drink." Caroline held out the travel cup. "It's warm out here."

"I'm not thirsty."

"Nina," Caroline warned.

The child glared at her, and she tensed. She didn't want to make a scene, but she also couldn't allow Nina to disrespect her.

So much for relaxing in the park. At least she'd been calm for three whole minutes. That had to count for something. Before she could respond, Seth slowed.

"Well, I'm thirsty." He smiled down at Nina. "And Spud's thirsty. And Liverwurst is, too. Let's all sit on the bench by the playground and have a drink."

"What will Spud drink out of?" Nina had bounced back to her cheerful self in two seconds flat.

"Your mom has a small bowl in her backpack. I'll fill it with water for him."

"Mommy always has what we need in her backpack, don't you, Mommy?" She sounded proud.

Her daughter was actually complimenting her? "I try, Nina."

"If you're hungry and want a granola bar, she's got 'em." Nina veered in the direction of the bench. They'd almost reached the playground.

"I'm okay for now," Seth said. "But thank you."

While he gave Nina a boost to sit on the bench, Caroline rooted around in the backpack until she found the collapsible bowl Seth had given her. She handed it to him. "Is this what you needed?"

"Yes." His fingers brushed hers during the exchange, and her skin tingled at his touch. Oh boy. Her attraction seemed to grow stronger every time they were together. And his quick smile was like a secret between them—the kind of look a husband would give his wife during an outing like this.

She really was reading too much into their time together. Sadly, she'd gotten so used to disappointing her ex-boyfriend, she'd forgotten little moments like these existed.

After Seth filled the bowl, the dogs took turns drinking water, and Caroline noted Nina was sipping from her travel cup. Spud finished drinking and parked himself in front of the girl, who began petting him.

"He's not alerting her, is he?" Caroline poked Seth's arm.

"No. He's staying close to her, like he's been trained. When he's wearing the vest, he knows he's on duty."

"Can I throw the ball to Spud?" Nina turned to ask Caroline.

"I'm not sure if it's allowed," she replied.

"But, Mommy, you know everything." Her eyelashes curled up, and the trust in her eyes reminded Caroline how much the girl looked up to her, even though they clashed at times.

"I don't know *everything*. But we have a dog expert here who should be able to answer your question."

Seth nodded. "Spud isn't allowed to play while he's wearing the vest."

"Am *I* allowed to play while he's wearing the vest?"

"Yes, you are. And after he gets his special certificate, he'll go with you everywhere, even to the playground."

"Can he go down the slide with me?"

"Nina!" Caroline's face flamed, and it wasn't due to the temperature. "No, he can't go down the slide. He's a dog."

"But it's fun," Nina whined.

Seth laughed. "Spud will wait for you to go down the slide."

"Can I go now?"

He glanced at Caroline for approval, and she figured if it was okay with him, it was okay with her.

"Let's check your reader first," Caroline said.

Nina unzipped the elastic waist pouch Caroline had purchased last week—a vast improvement over the clunky clip—and held up the reader. "See."

"Good numbers. Go ahead."

As Nina took off toward the slide, Caroline and Seth followed with the dogs.

"I'm glad you're letting her play." He gave her a sideways glance. "It gives me a chance to observe how Spud handles this situation."

"How is he supposed to handle it?" Caroline absentmindedly rubbed her forearm as she kept a watchful eye on Nina. Her dark brown curls popped up at the top of the slide, and she waved to them before sliding down.

"I'm letting him off leash," Seth said. "He should stay in her general vicinity."

"Is he allowed to be off leash in public?"

"In this situation, yes."

As soon as he unhooked the leash, the dog headed to the slide, where Nina squealed as she landed. She hugged his neck and petted his head, then ran around to climb the slide's ladder again. Spud stayed close, watching her until she was no longer in view. Then he ambled to the bottom of the slide as she squealed with delight.

"Do you know who Nina's teacher will be this fall?" Seth took Liverwurst's leash from her.

Hmm. That was an odd question. Caroline kept an eye on Nina as she responded. "Yes, she'll be in Mrs. Green's class."

"We should set up a time to talk to her about Spud. I'll explain to her what to expect with Spud and Nina, and the school can determine the best course of action on how they'll handle an alert when school is in session."

"I hadn't thought about the teacher needing to work with Spud." It all sounded so complicated.

"Don't worry. I'm used to these situations. I've talked to clients' employers and caregivers. Most people want to accommodate a service dog. They know how valuable they are for people who need them."

For some reason, his offer, his foresight about what Nina needed, were making her emotional. She wasn't going to cry, was she? *Get it together, Caroline!* She sniffed and squinted to see Nina. She wasn't on the slide. Where was she?

"Nina?" she cried out, her heart racing. "Where are you?"

Had she fallen? Passed out? Before panic could set in, Seth's hand on her arm caused her to still.

"She's over there." He pointed to the swing set. Then he studied her face. "Are you okay?"

"Yes." The relief flooding her core almost took her breath away. *I'm overreacting. I'm always overreacting.*

"Hey." His voice interrupted her thoughts.

"What?"

"She's not in danger. If she was, Spud would have come over to you. You can trust him. You can trust this process."

He might be right, but she didn't trust much of anything anymore. She swallowed, nodding. Her head knew he spoke the truth. But her heart struggled to accept it. Bad things happened when you least expected them. She didn't want to constantly be on guard, but what else could she do? Nina's health problems weren't going away.

Seth shifted to look into her eyes. "You're not alone. I'm here watching her. Spud's here. We're not going to let her down. I wouldn't let you down."

The barbed wire she'd installed around her heart fell away as if someone had taken wire cutters to it.

She hadn't realized until this moment how tired she was of being on high alert all the time. Was it even necessary to live like this—always worried? Now that they had the CGM and Spud?

"I appreciate that, Seth. And I know you wouldn't let me down. You've never let me down. I wish I could say the same about myself."

He tilted his head. "Shouldn't we leave the past alone? We were young. You were grieving. Let's let it go."

Let it go? Just like that? No. She didn't deserve it. "I thought you said we weren't ever going to be friends."

"I was wrong." A hint of a smile lifted his lips. "We *are* friends."

His words ripped down more of that barbed wire. Hope spread through her chest.

"Are you saying you forgive me?"

"If that's what you need, then, yes, I forgive you."

She hadn't realized how much she did need his forgiveness until the words came out of his mouth.

"I do need it," she whispered. "Thank you."

"Mr. Hudson!" Nina jogged to them with red cheeks. "Will you push me on the swings?"

"How high do you want to go?" He gave Caroline Liverwurst's leash, took Nina's hand and strolled to the swings with Spud.

"All the way to the moon!"

She wanted to call out for Nina to wait, to drink more water. But maybe Seth was right. If the CGM wasn't beeping and Spud wasn't alerting her, she shouldn't be worried, either.

Caroline stayed behind for a few moments. Seth had forgiven her. He'd declared they were friends. Since becoming a mom, she'd had no time to nurture friendships. And hanging out with Seth had become the highlight of each day. If he was offering friendship, she'd take it.

But what if she exploded the way she had years ago? She didn't want to drive him away, but she wasn't sure she could prevent it from happening again.

Caroline forced her feet forward. She didn't need to think about it now. She'd do her best to avoid having an epic meltdown and leave it at that.

* * *

"I need more coffee."

Seth stifled a snicker at Meena's tired face Friday morning as the squad ate breakfast around the lodge's kitchen table. What was it about the smell of sausage that made mornings better? Starting his day on the ranch with the squad was a welcome change from the morning commute in heavy Dallas traffic.

As much as he enjoyed these moments, he had a long list of things he'd been avoiding before the center could open. The crew had started installing Sheetrock throughout the pole barn. Seth looked forward to checking their progress every afternoon, but he'd be the first person to admit he'd been avoiding the technical stuff.

He needed to start working with the business software he'd purchased at Cooper's recommendation. While expensive, it would allow him to keep track of the dogs' boarding reservations, their vaccinations and special needs, playtime schedules and payment options, and it would even send emails to remind clients of upcoming boarding dates.

But to work with the software, he needed to install it on the new laptop, and both the laptop and software were still in boxes. Opening the boxes would only trigger hours of frustration he'd rather avoid.

"I'll get you a cup." Brody shoved his chair back to fetch his sister more coffee.

"What's got you so tired?" Seth asked her, craning his neck to check on Spud and Liverwurst. As usual, they'd found spots on the floor next to Butch. Liverwurst was grooming himself.

"I started thinking about this client call I had last week, and I had this vision to improve the flow of their main floor. Next thing I knew, I'd opened my design software and played around with a digital layout until three in the morning."

It didn't surprise him. His cousin tended to get creative bursts that took over her life. "At least you got your work done."

"No, that's the worst part." Meena dropped her forehead into her hands. Brody slid a steaming mug of coffee in front of her, and she lifted her head. "Thank you, Brody. You're the best."

He winked at her before reclaiming his seat.

She continued. "They didn't hire me to redesign their main floor. I only had a consulting video call to discuss their kitchen. Ugh. I love the company I work for, but this remote video consulting isn't working for me. I'm a hands-on designer, and this role feels like all talk, no action."

Seth met Brody's gaze, then glanced at Cooper and Hayden. Lillian got up and put her arm around Meena's shoulders. "I'm sorry you're frustrated."

Meena twisted for a brief hug. "Thanks, Lil. I know I'm being dramatic. It's fine. I'll be fine."

If she said she'd be fine, Seth figured she'd be fine. But Lillian's frown made him question if he was wrong.

"Maybe it's time to renovate your own cabin, Meena." Lillian sat back in her chair while Jonah kicked his legs in the bouncy seat on the floor.

"My cabin?" Meena blinked twice. Then she picked up her mug, blew across the top and took a sip. "Yes. I could renovate my cabin." She had a faraway look in her eyes, but she didn't sound excited.

Cooper caught Seth's attention and raised his eyebrows as if to ask what was going on. Seth shrugged. Beat him.

"Hey, Meena," Seth said, "if you're up to it later, why don't you come with me to the center? You can go through the house with me. Show me what I need to buy for decorations."

"When are you going?" She yawned. From the looks of it, she needed a nap more than anything.

"This afternoon."

"Text me thirty minutes before you plan on leaving."

"Will do."

"Have you gotten started on the new software?" Cooper

sliced into a sausage patty. Unlike Seth, he actually liked technology and had no trouble figuring out software without spending hours watching YouTube videos.

"The boxes are sitting in my cabin. I haven't opened them." Seth had never thought he and Meena had much in common, but now that he thought about it, he liked hands-on work the best, too. It wasn't that he didn't understand how to use software. He simply found no joy in doing it. And given all the things the new program would be tracking, setting it all up was sure to strain his brain.

"Want me to come over and look at it?" Cooper asked.

"Would you?" With Cooper's help, setting it up would be a breeze. Seth polished off a slice of toast, suddenly feeling better about his day.

"Sure."

"I thought you were gathering grass samples from the pastures all week to have analyzed, Coop." Brody set his silverware on top of his empty plate.

"I've already gotten samples from the bulls' pasture. I sure am glad you moved them to graze with the cows. I didn't want to face a bull in there." Coop stood, grabbing his utensils. "I'll get to the other pastures soon. Gathering samples doesn't take all day, bro."

Brody made an impatient sound. "Yeah, but we need the data so we can determine the nutrition needs of all the herds before winter."

"Winter's a long way off." Cooper took his dishes to the sink, sprayed them and placed them in the dishwasher.

"It'll be here before you know it..."

"You're quiet." Seth glanced at Hayden, who hadn't made a peep throughout the meal.

He glanced up from shoveling scrambled eggs into his mouth. After finishing the bite, he pointed to his chest. "Who, me?"

"Yeah, you. Is something wrong?"

"Nothing's wrong. I'm mentally going through my list for the day."

Seth didn't put much thought into how Hayden spent his days. Seth had acted as a ranch hand with him and the guys over the summers, so he knew what caring for cattle entailed. But something told him Hayden's job was more complicated than they gave him credit for.

"What's on the list?" Seth figured it would involve fixing fences and checking cattle.

"There's some fence down, and one of the heifers has a foot fungus. I've got a vet coming out next week for vaccinations, and she said she'll check on it then. I'm worried about how the calves of the new Simmental bull we bred with the Herefords are going to do once they're born. And I probably should purchase a few new feeders for the steer pen."

Seth blinked, not knowing how to respond. If anyone could handle all that, Hayden could. His brother had spent years as the ranch manager for a different cattle operation.

"The calves will be fine," Brody said loudly from across the kitchen. He worked every morning with Hayden and the other ranch hands. "Better than fine. Trust me on this."

Hayden's jaw clenched, and he shoved another bite into his mouth.

"Are you ready to install the software?" Cooper stood near the hall leading to the mudroom.

"Yep. Be right there." Seth took care of his plate and called the dogs, then he joined Cooper outside. Birds chirped as they strode down the lane to the cabins, and the blue sky held puffy clouds. Liverwurst and Spud trotted ahead of them.

"How is Spud doing with the little girl?" Cooper asked.

"He and Nina have a special bond." Seth couldn't help but smile. "He's quick at finding the saliva samples, and he obeys her commands. Plus, he loves all the attention she gives him. It's going better than I'd hoped."

"That's good. I'm glad to hear it. And how's her mother?"

"Caroline's fine." A sliver of anxiety colored his words. He'd been thinking about her more than he wanted to. Ever since the park, when he'd told her they were friends, his attitude toward her had shifted. He'd been paying more attention to her every move each night as Nina and Spud worked together. He'd always thought she was beautiful. Lately, he'd been able to admit they'd both matured. "I, um, kind of changed my mind about being friends."

"Oh, so you two are friends again." Cooper's voice lilted.

"Yeah."

"And just how friendly are you?"

"As friendly as a guy who's training a service dog for her kid can be." He didn't mean to snap, but liking Caroline was new to him after more than a decade holding a grudge. He didn't appreciate the insinuation that they were a couple.

"Are all your trainees' moms as pretty as she is?" Cooper's knowing grin made him pick up the pace.

"I don't know. I don't usually work with clients' mothers."

Cooper had no trouble matching his strides. "Do you see a future with her?"

"No." The word shot out before he even considered the question. Did he see a future with her? "I don't know. I think she's a good mom. She's a hard worker. We get along—always did."

"But?" The cabins came into view.

He sighed. "She thought the worst of me once. What's to say she won't do it again?"

Cooper nodded. They reached Seth's porch, and he waited for his cousin and the dogs to get inside before joining them.

"How much longer does Spud need until he can live there?" Cooper toed off his shoes and headed into the living room, where the dogs were already curling up on their dog beds under the front window.

"Another week. Maybe two. I have to run him through the

certification tests. I wish Kylie could be there for it. She's familiar with the test and has helped me with them in the past." Seth took off his boots, too, and pulled out his pocketknife. He went to the pile of boxes and began slicing through the packing tape.

"Okay. Another week or two and then you won't be hanging out there every night." Cooper motioned with his fingers for Seth to hand him the first box he opened. Seth did.

His words should have brought Seth relief, but all he felt was disappointment. He'd been enjoying their time together. He looked forward to spending every evening with Caroline and Nina. Working with an impressive service dog like Spud fulfilled him.

His summer routine was about to change. After Spud was certified, the dog would live with Nina. No more training. And by the end of summer, the boarding center would be open for business.

Everything would be in place as it should be. He'd have a new career. Nina would have a service dog. And Caroline would have peace of mind.

None of it made him as happy as it should.

"I keep forgetting." Seth shook his head. Spud couldn't move in at any time, not with the daycare situation. "Caroline's looking for a babysitter for Nina. It would be full-time until school starts, and then she'd need a sitter after school. I meant to ask Meena and Lillian if they know of anyone who'd be interested."

Cooper had pulled out an instruction manual. He didn't glance up as he flipped through it. "Lillian knows all the church people. Text her."

"Do you mind if I call her now?"

"Go for it. Where's your laptop?"

"It's over there. Still in the box." He pointed to the floor near the couch.

"I'm setting this up."

"Good. You're way better at it than I am."

Seth took the opportunity to call Lillian, who answered after one ring.

"Hey, Lillian, do you know of anyone in Fairwood who might be interested in babysitting Nina?"

"What do you have in mind? A teenager on a Saturday night or—"

"No, someone willing to watch her full-time until school starts. Then it would be after school and on school holidays."

"I thought Nina went to Happy Time Daycare."

"She does, but it's not the right environment for Spud."

"I see what you mean. All those kids would be a distraction." He liked that he didn't have to explain things to Lillian. She got it. "I can't think of anyone off the top of my head."

Disappointment settled.

"Oh, wait. What about Fran Bolenski?"

"Who?"

"Fran's an older woman from church. She lives on Birch Street in a duplex. She's lonely and loves kids. I'll text you her number."

"Thanks, Lillian." His mood improved. "I appreciate it."

"You're welcome."

As soon as the call ended, he got the text with Fran's information. He immediately texted it to Caroline. Talk to Fran about babysitting Nina.

He thought about the Friday night rodeos all summer in a nearby town. It would be fun to go to one with her and Nina. He shot her another text. What are you doing tonight?

His phone chimed. I have plans with Dad.

There went that idea. Before he could talk himself out of it, he texted back.

Want to go to the rodeo next Friday? Spud and Nina, too?

He waited for a reply, and none came. He shouldn't feel let down. But he did.

For the next couple of hours, Cooper installed the software on the new laptop and the two of them figured out the basics. Then Seth's phone chimed. A text from Caroline. It simply said yes.

"Must have been some text to make you grin like that." Cooper set the laptop aside.

"I'm taking Caroline and Nina to the rodeo next Friday."

Cooper had a contemplative air about him.

"You don't think it's a good idea." His good mood took a dive.

"If you're into Caroline and you don't think she'll hurt you, I say go for it. But you know she comes with a kid who has extra needs. Be careful."

A month ago, Seth would have told him he didn't need to be careful, that he'd never get close to her. But now? He'd be wise to keep Cooper's advice in mind. He was already smitten with the little girl. He couldn't afford to fall in love with Caroline and lose them both.

Chapter Seven

"Are you sure this is wise?" Caroline held Spud's leash the following Friday while Seth carried Nina on his shoulders. Dust kicked up in the air as people thronged around them. Honky-tonk music played over loudspeakers, and the bright lights of food trucks provided a colorful backdrop on their way to the stands.

She wasn't sure why she'd agreed to come to the rodeo with Seth. Ever since Nina's diagnosis, she typically made excuses to avoid crowds. Seemed dangerous to put her sweet girl in situations where Caroline might get distracted and miss her symptoms. Memories from a year ago, of being in the hospital with Nina hooked up to tubes and wires, made her shudder. That had been before she'd been diagnosed with diabetes, before she'd gotten the CGM.

"We have to make sure Spud can handle crowds," Seth said. "These situations will be part of his life from now on."

Not if she didn't take Nina to rodeos, they wouldn't be. She instantly regretted the thought. Didn't her daughter deserve to have fun like everyone else? Seth had gone out of his way to make sure tonight went smoothly, and she'd appreciated his patience as he spoke with the ticket office employees about allowing Spud inside. Since the dog was wearing a vest that said Medical Alert Dog in Training, the rodeo staff had allowed it.

A high-pitched squeal erupted from Nina, and Caroline's heart thumped. What was wrong? She shifted to look up at the girl. She was pointing toward the arena, where cowgirls and cowboys were saddled up near the gate as they waited for the events to begin.

She heaved a sigh of relief. Nothing was wrong. Nina was excited. That was all. After a tough week when she'd had to call the daycare twice after the CGM app beeped for several minutes, she supposed it made sense she was on high alert. The daycare employee had assured her Nina was fine, but it bothered her they'd taken so long to give her juice. Didn't they realize she could fall into a diabetic coma? And land in the hospital again?

"Look, Mr. Hudson! I see the ponies!"

"You'll be seeing a lot more of them when we find our seats." Seth shot a smile Caroline's way, sending flutters to her stomach. He sure was handsome. "How about we grab a bite to eat first? Anything sound good, Nina?"

"Ice cream!"

Seth chuckled, but Caroline didn't. Nina knew she wasn't supposed to have sugar. "Let's find something safe for you to eat." She'd have to calculate how much insulin to give her, too. She'd gotten good at estimating doses.

"Could she have ice cream if it's sugar-free?" Seth grew serious.

"Yes, but I highly doubt any of these places offer it."

"Let's check before ruling it out." He led the way to a food truck advertising soft-serve ice cream.

Caroline noted how easily Spud maneuvered the crowds. His easygoing panting made her feel better about this outing. Spud and Seth were helping her daughter, too.

A long line of people waited to order, but she moved around them to see the menu and was surprised to see they did have a sugar-free option.

"They have sugar-free vanilla, Nina." Caroline wasn't used to looking up to talk to her. Nina's joyful expression went straight to her heart. If it wasn't for Seth, her baby would be home right now, watching an animated movie for the fifteenth time. Getting out tonight was good for them both. “Do you want a dish?”

“Yes, Mommy!”

“Okay, I’ll get your insulin ready first.” Caroline touched Seth’s arm, trying not to think about those hard muscles. “Can you bring her down so I can give her the insulin?”

“Sure thing.” He carefully twisted Nina in his arms and set her on her feet.

“We’ll be right back. I see a restroom in that building.” Caroline pointed to the left.

“Meet me here when you’re finished. Take Spud with you.”

Caroline nodded. Nina held her hand as she chattered about how much she loved the rodeo and how she couldn’t wait to get ice cream. Once they reached the bathroom, it didn’t take long for Caroline to wash her hands and give Nina the insulin shot. Spud was a trouper, panting and smiling as women oohed and ahhed over him as they came and went.

“Can I hold Spud’s leash now, Mommy?” Nina asked as they exited the restroom.

“Sure. He’s your super dog, right?”

“Right.”

“Remember what Mr. Hudson told you.”

“I remember. He has to heel.”

“Unless?” Caroline paused, holding her hand.

“Unless he’s wiggly and licking me.” That meant the dog sensed a problem.

“Good job.” Caroline and Nina navigated the crowds to get back to Seth. “Oh, I see him.”

“Me too!” Nina surged forward, but Caroline’s grip on her hand stopped her.

“Slow down. There are too many people here for us to get separated.”

Nina slowed her pace, and when they reached Seth, he had his hand behind his back.

"I've got something for you," he said to Nina.

"What is it?" She sounded breathless.

"Ta-da!" He produced a pink straw cowboy hat for her, complete with feathers and sequins. A five-year-old girl's dream.

"My own cowboy hat!" Nina turned to Caroline. "Look, it's sparkly. Can I keep it?"

His thoughtfulness touched her, but it concerned her, too. Seth showed Nina so much kindness, and her daughter already thought of him as her hero. How would Nina react after Spud moved in and Seth no longer came over at night? She'd probably be crushed. Caroline might be, as well.

"It's perfect. So pink and pretty." Caroline gave her a warm smile as Seth placed it on her head. "What do you say to Mr. Hudson?"

"Thank you!" Nina, still holding the leash, wrapped her arms around his legs. Seth chuckled and hugged her back.

"You're welcome. Let's get that ice cream." They joined the end of the line, and Nina asked Seth about the rodeo. He explained about the barrel racing, bull riding and rodeo clowns.

"Clowns?" Nina flashed a grimace. "George went to a circus and a clown scared him."

"Who's George?" Seth asked.

"He's at daycare. He colors all his pictures with a blue crayon."

Caroline had heard about George more than once. Nina tended to go on and on about the kids at daycare.

"These clowns are to distract the bulls and keep the cowboys safe." Seth inched forward with Nina and Spud next to him as the line moved. He turned to Caroline. "Speaking of daycare, did you ever talk to Fran Bolenski?"

"I keep getting her answering machine. I assume it's not a cell phone. I wish she'd return my calls. I don't know how comfortable I am with someone who isn't responsive."

"Maybe she's out of town."

"Maybe."

Soon they'd placed their order and headed to the stands. When they'd found seats, Nina plowed into her ice cream, and Caroline dipped her spoon into a cup of soft-serve swirl. Seth had opted for a strawberry sundae, and he'd gotten Spud a small cup of ice cream, too. The dog was licking it up in a hurry.

"Mommy, look at how fast Spud ate his ice cream." Nina pointed her spoon at the dog, who was determined to get every last drop from the Styrofoam cup.

"Watch yourself!" Caroline reached for her tilting dish.

"I got it." She righted it and dipped her spoon into the melting mess. "Yummy! I *love, love, love* ice cream."

Soon, the announcer requested everyone stand for the "Star-Spangled Banner," then the first event commenced. Caroline found the wipes in her backpack and handed one to Nina. Then Seth hauled the girl onto his lap, with Spud sitting beside them.

As Caroline took in the sight of her daughter on Seth's lap, something shifted inside her. The sense that everything depended on her alone—Nina's safety, her happiness—no longer had a vise grip around her. And it was all because of Seth.

Caroline relaxed into her seat, took in the magenta and orange sunset, and watched the first barrel racer enter the arena. This might be the last time she had a night like this with Seth. She was going to enjoy it.

"Is she okay?" Caroline's hand touched Seth's forearm, and he liked the feel of her slender fingers on his skin a little too much.

"She's asleep." Seth shifted Nina, still on his lap, as the final event of the rodeo began. Bull riding had always been his favorite, but with Nina on his lap and Caroline touching his arm, a spacecraft could have landed in the arena and he wouldn't have noticed.

Tonight had been amazing for all the wrong reasons.

Instead of watching the barrel racing, he'd been caught up

in Nina's excitement as she raved about how fast the "ponies" ran. He'd sneaked peeks at Caroline's profile as she gasped at how close to the barrels they raced. And he'd monitored Spud, who was behaving exactly as he should. Sitting quietly, occasionally sniffing Nina and not causing a fuss.

"I can take her if she's getting heavy," Caroline said.

"This bitty thing? I haul bags of dog food heavier than her. She's fine where she is."

She nodded, settling back into her seat once more. "It was kind of you to buy her the hat. She'll never want to take it off."

It had been a no-brainer. He'd spotted it for sale in a booth as they'd walked in. "She should have a cowgirl hat."

"And pink with sparkles."

"Of course. Nina likes pink and sparkles."

Her smile grew wider.

"Man, Caroline, you're pretty when you smile."

The smile vanished. She ducked her chin.

Dumb. Why did you compliment her? You're friends. Just friends.

"Thanks." The vulnerability in her eyes made his stomach tumble. He wanted to touch her cheek, run the backs of his fingers down it. Cup her chin and kiss her.

Whoa. Get your head on straight.

Nina's soft sigh as she slept brought his thoughts back to the rodeo. He pointed to the arena. "I wonder how long number twenty-three will stay on."

Caroline leaned forward. "Eight seconds, I hope."

"If he's skilled enough."

The gate opened, and the bull came out doing its best to buck the rider off. Unfortunately for the rider, the bull succeeded. A rodeo clown tried to distract the beast while the rider sprang to his feet. Caroline grabbed Seth's hand and gripped it with both of hers, never taking her eyes off the scene. The rider climbed the fence right before the bull charged him.

"I thought the bull was going to trample him." She must have realized she was holding his hand, because she dropped it like he had a skin disease. Seth missed her touch. Liked that her first impulse was reaching for him.

"He's quick on his feet." He didn't know why he said that.

"I don't know why they willingly put themselves in danger like that. Do they have a death wish or something?" She rapidly patted her chest and turned to him.

"They love the challenge."

"Challenge? I can think of a thousand things I'd rather do than get gored by a bull." She grimaced.

"Actually, I can, too. It's never been my thing."

"That's because you're sensible."

Sensible? Was that a good thing? He wasn't a wuss, if that's what she was implying. "I'm not scared."

"I didn't say you were," she said. Then she faced him, her expression clear, looking all of eighteen again. "What's the scariest thing you've done?"

He thought about it. "Moving here."

"Really? I thought you loved Fairwood. You used to talk about how you wished you lived on your grandparents' ranch. But I guess I ruined that for you, too."

"You didn't ruin it for me," he said quietly. "I found a job in Dallas that I loved."

"Hmm. Why'd you move back to the ranch, then?" Her eyebrows drew together. "Did you always want to open the dog-boarding center?"

"I never planned to quit training service dogs, but when we inherited the ranch, I realized how burned out I was. The constant traveling made me dread each new client. I didn't know I was going to open a dog-boarding center until recently. That's why moving back scared me. I wasn't sure about the future."

"Moving back scared me, too. After my mom died and Dad

sold the farm, Fairwood didn't feel like home to me. If it wasn't for Nina, I'd have never come back."

"Has it been difficult? The memories?"

"No. I thought it might be hard, but it hasn't been. Dad's content working for the post office. In his downtime, he's off fishing and hunting with his buddies. And I only have good memories of my mother. I wish she were still here. She'd know what to do when I have questions about Nina."

"You're doing a good job. You're a good mom." His voice had grown husky. He cleared his throat.

"I'm too wound up." Her expression grew serious as she stared out toward the arena. "I almost said no to coming tonight. It felt overwhelming—taking Nina out in a crowd, worrying about her having an episode with her blood sugar. I get this panicky feeling inside sometimes and I'm afraid I'll burst."

"Understandable." He nodded. "I'd worry, too. But, for the record, I'm glad you said yes."

"I'm glad I did, too." Her eyes shined with gratitude and appreciation. Familiar feelings overrode the warnings he'd been giving himself. Warm, romantic feelings. The kind that made him want to hold her hand, put his arm around her shoulders and kiss her.

"Looks like the final rider's coming up." He practically choked on the words. They'd missed most of the bull riding, and he didn't care. He didn't want this night to end, but he needed it to end soon.

He was getting too close to Caroline Bright, and if she hurt him like she did last time, he couldn't just move to another town. He'd have a business to run. And he wouldn't leave the squad, not now that they were finally together again.

If he wasn't careful, he'd repeat the mistakes of the past, and he'd only have himself to blame.

Chapter Eight

"I'm so glad I reached you. I've been calling your home phone number." Caroline wore earbuds as she walked down the sidewalk on her lunch break the following Monday. Meena, Seth's cousin, had approached her after church yesterday with Fran's cell phone number. Caroline remembered Meena, a beautiful brunette with animated blue eyes and a bounce in her step, and appreciated the kind gesture. Years ago, she'd met her and Kylie once, but she'd never met the rest of Seth's siblings and cousins. The fact that Meena was treating her like a friend meant a lot.

Fran cleared her throat. "I'm in Idaho with my daughter."

"Oh, are you two vacationing?" Caroline kept her pace brisk. The weather was perfect—not too hot with low humidity. She tried to get outside for lunch as often as possible. Today, she'd packed a turkey wrap sandwich. Her stomach growled in anticipation.

"No, honey, I missed my grandbabies—Hunter and Maddie—and figured I'd take a road trip."

Two points in Fran's favor. She loved kids and could drive.

"I got your number from Meena Hudson—"

"How is Meena? I keep telling her to give my Alex a call, but she's been too shy. If I could snap a photo of her, I'd send it to him. I'm sure they'd hit it off next time he's in town."

Meena didn't strike Caroline as the shy type. "Who's Alex?"

"My son. A bachelor. It's time for him to settle down. Say, you don't happen to be single, do you?"

"Um, yes, but that's not why I'm calling." She clutched her lunch bag as she hurried across the street to the park. The gazebo was just up ahead. "I'm wondering if you babysit at all?"

Fran's chuckle lasted a few moments. "Of course I babysit. I'd babysit my grandbabies every day if given the chance. I love kids. Why?"

"My daughter, Nina, will be starting school this fall. But she has type 1 diabetes and is getting a service dog."

"A service dog? She's not blind, is she?"

"No, it's not a guide dog. It's a medical alert dog. He can sense when her blood sugar gets low."

"Well, I'll be. I didn't know dogs could do that. How does he know?"

Caroline didn't have all day to explain, but she forced herself to be polite. "Through scent recognition. Anyhow, his trainer, Seth Hudson—"

"Is he the quiet one I see around town with the giant beagle?"

"I suppose. It's an American foxhound, though."

"That dog sure is cute. I was telling Jackie at church…" Fran continued with a story about a skunk and a beagle, and Caroline tried to find an opening to interject.

"Yes, well, Nina's currently going to Happy Time Daycare while I work, and it's not the right environment for a service dog."

Fran made a tsk-tsk sound. "I should hope not. All those kids trying to ride the poor thing like a pony. I wouldn't wish that on any furry friend."

Good, she seemed to understand the issue.

"I'm trying to find a sitter. It would be full-time until school starts, then it would only be weekday afternoons and all day on school breaks."

"One little girl, you said?" Fran asked.

Caroline's hopes rose. "Yes. But you would have to administer insulin shots. I would walk you through it, don't worry."

She tried to breathe normally, but it proved difficult. So much was riding on finding a babysitter for Nina. *God, I need some help here.*

"Shots?" Fran asked. Caroline prepared herself for a letdown. "Honey, I was a phlebotomist before I had my babies." Her throaty chuckle lasted forever. "I have no problem giving shots."

As much as Caroline wished she could hire her on the spot, caution overrode the urge. "Could I come over and meet you sometime this week? So we could discuss this further?"

"No."

"Why not?" What had she said? Had she completely turned her off to the idea of watching Nina? Maybe the woman enjoyed her freedom. Caroline couldn't fault her for that.

"I'll be in Idaho staying with Anne and the kiddos until the middle of August. But after that, why don't you bring your sweet pea over and we'll talk?"

Mid-August. Caroline took a seat on the bench in the gazebo as disappointment crushed her. Could she wait that long for Spud to move in? And what if Fran wasn't a good fit? She'd still need to find a babysitter—and no one seemed to be available. Her coworkers had given her names, and she'd called them all, with no success.

"Let's put it on the calendar." Caroline set the lunch bag on the bench and swiped her phone to the calendar app. "What day should I bring Nina over?"

After setting a date and time, Caroline thanked her. Before she could end the call, Fran spoke. "Oh, and honey, I'm going to send you pictures of my Alex. The next time he's in town, you two can get to know each other. He's a good son, handsome as can be and he likes kids and dogs. You're practically made for each other."

"Um, I'd better not."

"Don't say no. I'll text you photos right now. You'll see. He's perfect for you."

Considering Fran had never met her, Caroline didn't believe that to be true. "Okay. Goodbye."

Finally. Caroline shoved the phone back in her purse and opened the lunch bag. Just as she was about to bite into the turkey wrap, her phone dinged. Texts from Fran. She opened them and snorted a laugh. Seven photos? This woman had never met her yet was sending pictures of her son—admittedly good-looking. The remaining photos were of a toddler boy and baby girl, Fran holding the toddler, a woman with the baby—her daughter?—and an off-center picture of a steering wheel.

The phone dinged again. Fran texted. Sorry about the last one. Took it on accident. Send me a picture of you, and I'll pass it on to Alex.

Wasn't happening. She ignored the texts and bit into the wrap. While things were headed in the right direction on the babysitter front, she wished everything could be wrapped up with a tidy bow. She hated the uncertainty of not having a babysitter. She wanted Spud to live with them now. Today.

She bit into a carrot stick. Last night, she'd woken three times to check on Nina. The CGM had beeped twice before Nina went to bed, and Caroline had been on high alert. Thinking about the lack of sleep made her tired.

Could she talk to Seth about allowing Spud to move in before she had a babysitter?

She winced. Didn't Spud have to pass a test first to make it official that he was a medical alert dog? She usually had a handle on what needed to happen, but today, everything jumbled together in her brain.

Opening an app on her phone, she reviewed the running checklists she kept and scrolled down to the one labeled "Spud." Yes, the dog had to be certified by Seth before moving in.

Another text dinged, and she checked her phone. Brent

Thompson, her boss. You're signed up for the one-day training we discussed. Two links arrived bing-bang-bing.

Frowning, she popped the final bite of the turkey wrap in her mouth. What training? She didn't remember discussing it. After clicking on the first link, she scanned the syllabus. Touted as hands-on, interactive training in the administration and development of client legal matters, the workshop was being held in Cheyenne, scheduled for a Saturday two weeks from now. The second link was a hotel reservation for that night.

Her stomach soured. How could she leave Nina for an entire day on a Saturday? The daycare was only open on weekdays. She absolutely could *not* spend the night in Cheyenne. What if something happened to Nina?

Zipping her lunch bag closed, she tried to remember when she'd discussed this with her boss. Nothing came to mind… unless…well, they *had* talked about continuous education during her interview. Brent had been adamant the firm would pay for classes so they could get her on the fast track to becoming a paralegal.

She hadn't expected the classes to start this soon or to be out of town. Maybe it would be offered remotely and she could stay here and take the class online.

If not? The only person she could ask to watch Nina was her dad, and as much as she loved him, she worried that Nina's reader would go off and he wouldn't know what to do.

What about Seth?

Caroline hauled herself to her feet. No. She wouldn't ask him. They were friends, but the way she was feeling lately veered past friendship, and she didn't have a future with him. Not with her life the way it was. She'd only drive him away with her lists and paranoia about Nina.

After tossing the empty baggies in the trash, she strolled out of the gazebo to return to work.

The rodeo had been a gift—one he surely didn't even know

he'd given her. She'd felt young and hopeful and happy for the first time in years. Her life had become a series of anxiety-filled days full of to-do lists and the feeling of never being caught up. But the rodeo had allowed her to pause. How she'd relished the brief break. A chance to sit and watch the sunset and enjoy Nina's wonder at the horses and have an easy conversation with a man she'd been friends with back when she wasn't a single mom in way over her head with everything.

She'd always been an overthinker. It had gotten worse as the years went by. And she didn't think she could turn it off. Didn't really want to. If she did, she'd put Nina at risk.

No one would ever be as diligent as she was when it came to Nina's health.

As if on cue, the CGM's app on her phone began beeping. *Great.* She checked the app—low blood sugar. How long would it take the daycare to give her daughter juice or candy? Five minutes? Ten? Far too long in her mind. Should she call them?

They'd gotten snippy the last time she'd called. If after five minutes, the alert didn't stop, she was calling the daycare, no matter what.

Caroline paid no attention to the perfect weather as she power walked back to work and mentally reviewed the texts and calls she'd taken before lunch. She'd add a reminder on her day planner to meet with Fran in mid-August. She'd also talk to Brent—who was out of town for the week—about canceling the training session in Cheyenne and finding something she could do from home. And tonight, when Seth arrived, she needed him to explain exactly what needed to happen before Spud could live with them.

Usually, rehashing her to-do list helped make her feel calm. But today, it only riled her up. Thankfully, the app stopped beeping. The daycare must be on top of it.

Why did she have the feeling one of these days her calendar and to-do list would spin out of control? And like she'd done in the past, she'd blow up and take it out on someone else. She'd be helpless to prevent the horrific fallout from happening.

The bottom line? She didn't trust herself around Seth. She'd already hurt him once. She couldn't live with herself if she hurt him again.

In and out. Seth hoped there wouldn't be a line at the post office Monday afternoon. It would be closing soon, and he had to sign for a certified mail package—the legal documents for Hudson K-9 Center. He'd have stopped by earlier, but he'd been enjoying working with Spud, and he'd been ignoring the paperwork for the center. Wasn't he supposed to be focusing on the new business and putting training service dogs behind him?

As he pulled open the door, a bell rang above it. After this he'd head to Caroline's for another training session. Little did she know they'd be discussing Spud's final tests, which he hoped to perform on Friday. Then Spud would graduate from his training vest to the pink medical alert dog vest he'd purchased. If Caroline approved, he wanted to take her and Nina back to the lodge for a celebratory meal afterward and introduce them to the squad.

But was Caroline ready for the dog? While Spud had alerted her several times over the course of their sessions, Seth had always given her a heads-up that Spud was sensing something. He'd have to trust she was ready. He needed to get his head back where it belonged—on opening the center.

He strode to the counter. No customers waited in line. He heaved a sigh of relief.

"How can I help you?" Ken Bright glanced up from behind the counter and visibly faltered. "Oh, Seth. It's you. I've been meaning to stop by. Heard you're opening a dog-boarding center in town."

"Hi, Ken." Seth held out his hand. He'd always liked Caroline's father, but he wasn't sure how the man felt about him after all this time. "Yes, the center should be open around the end of August."

"Good, good." Ken's throat worked as he swallowed. "I'm sorry for...you know...everything that happened after the funeral."

"Don't mention it." Seth shifted his weight. This conversation had barely begun and he was already unbearably uncomfortable.

"Hear me out. I've felt bad for years about how Caroline treated you and for not contacting you immediately after you drove away."

"You'd just buried your wife. I think you can let the guilt go." As Seth said it, the truth of the words hit him. Logically, he'd known Caroline and Ken were grieving, but he hadn't really grasped how differently they'd have reacted to the tragedy if they hadn't already been mourning. "Besides, you called and told me what happened."

"We let you down, Seth. I'm sorry."

Ken's words healed an open wound he hadn't realized still festered inside him. "Thank you."

"I appreciate all you're doing for our Nina—and for Caroline. The diagnosis has been tough on them both, and this service dog will make a big difference."

"I'm glad to do it. Nina deserves an extra helper." An idea came to him, but he hesitated, unsure if he should run it by Caroline first. Eh, he'd chance it. "I plan on testing Spud and Nina this Friday evening. If he passes, he'll no longer be in training."

"Really?" Ken brightened. "Will he be allowed to live with them?"

"Not yet." Seth explained the daycare situation. "Why don't you come over for the final testing? I could use your help for some of the tests."

"I'd like that. And if it's all right with you, I'd like to stop by the new training center soon. See what you've got planned over there."

"That would be great. Stop by anytime."

"Now, what can I do for you?" Ken beamed.

A few minutes later, Seth carried the package to his truck. The windows were rolled down, and both dogs sat in the back seat with their tongues out, panting. In the driver's seat, he opened the package and took out the documents. Everything appeared to be in order. Legally, he was all set to open the center—after the renovations were completed and it passed inspection, of course.

As he drove to Caroline's, a feeling of accomplishment came over him. Although he hadn't been spending as much time on it as he should, the center was on track. He and Cooper had set up the software, and thanks to his cousin's tech skills, Seth understood how each part of the program worked. From payment options and scheduling, to inputting individual dogs' medical data, he'd be on top of the business side of things.

Now that Spud's training was almost finished, Seth wouldn't be spending all this time with Caroline and Nina. While it should please him, it didn't. He'd grown close to the single mom. Too close. In fact, the rodeo had brought him right back to being eighteen, except this time, they were both adults.

At the rodeo, Caroline had been relaxed. An easy smile had replaced the tightness that usually lined her mouth. He'd liked having Nina on his lap. He'd liked having Caroline by his side.

But he couldn't fall into that trap again. Caroline and Nina weren't his and never would be. He just didn't trust that she'd believe the best in him if something went wrong. Maybe she'd changed, but from the way she worried and planned for every possible emergency, he guessed she hadn't.

So why couldn't he stop thinking about her?

He parked in her drive. As far as he knew, she still hadn't told Nina she was adopted. School would start in the fall. Wouldn't it be better for the kid to know her father wasn't in the picture because she was adopted rather than think he didn't want her?

Maybe he was reading too much into it. Nina might not think about it at all. She was a smart little thing, though, and he guessed she'd thought about it many times.

Seth parked the truck on the street in front of Caroline's house, let out the dogs and climbed the porch steps. After a few knocks, she opened the door, and her big smile practically punched him in the chest.

She was beautiful. A take-charge woman. A worrywart. And all he could think about was pulling her into his arms and kissing her. Hadn't he spent the past ten minutes convincing himself they were all wrong for each other?

"Oh good, you're here." She waved him inside, shutting the door behind him. "I have some questions for you."

He had questions, too. Like did she ever think about him as more than a friend? Did she have feelings for him? Could she see a boyfriend—or husband—in her future?

All the questions were inappropriate. He didn't fully trust her, and she didn't trust him. Their friendship might have resumed, but it was new and tender like the bud of a spring flower.

Still…they'd both grown up. He needed to remember that.

"Mr. Hudson!" Nina barreled to him, and he caught her up in his arms, lifting her off her feet.

"Howdy, Nina." He couldn't help smiling at her as he set her back down.

"I made you something!" Her hazel eyes twinkled with excitement.

"You did?"

"I'll go get it!" She raced down the hallway.

Caroline crouched to pet Spud. "I've been wondering about what needs to happen before Spud can officially be Nina's service dog."

"We must be on the same page, then, because I planned on talking to you about it tonight."

"He'll be my doggy tonight?" Nina rushed back into the

room clutching a paper. Her eyes were impossibly round and full of hope.

Seth crouched to her level. “Not tonight. But soon. If your mom’s okay with it, I’ll put him through the Canine Good Citizen test Friday night.”

“Friday! Yay! Yay!” Nina hopped up and down, then controlled herself and thrust the paper to him. “It’s for you.”

Seth took it in both hands. She’d drawn stick figures of him, Caroline, her and the two dogs. His heart puddled at the sweet drawing.

“You drew this for me?” he asked.

She nodded, suddenly shy.

“Come here.” He gestured for her to come close, and he pulled her into a hug, kissing the top of her head. “Thank you. This means so much to me. I’m going to put it on my fridge so I can always look at it.”

“It’s you and me and Mommy and Spud and Liverwurst.” She turned toward the kitchen as Spud and Liverwurst walked away. “I’d better see what they’re doing.” Nina hummed as she followed the dogs into the kitchen.

Seth set the paper on the nearest end table, then turned to Caroline. “I ran into your dad at the post office. I invited him to join us Friday. We could use an extra person as part of the testing.”

“And what did he say?”

“He wants to come.”

“That wasn’t all he said, was it?” The vulnerability in her eyes lowered his defenses.

“He said more. About the past. Don’t worry. We’re good.”

She bit her lower lip and nodded. Nina and the dogs came back into the room.

“So, Nina—” Seth forced an upbeat note in his voice “—over the next couple of days, you and I are going to be walking through each and every test Spud needs to pass. Are you up for it?"

"Yes!" She was petting Spud. "I can't wait for Spuddy to live with me."

"Your mom and I have to discuss that, too," Seth said. "Spud might have to wait a while before he can move in. You'll have to be patient."

"I don't want to wait. My doggy loves me, don't you?" She pressed her cheek against his back and kept one arm around him. The dog turned to her and licked her face. She giggled.

"Nina, why don't you take Spud to your room for a minute?" Caroline hitched her chin.

"Okay. Come on, you, too, Liverwurst." The girl talked to the dogs all the way to her room.

"I called Fran Bolenski about babysitting." Caroline was chipping the polish from her thumbnail. A sure sign she was stressed. "She's out of town until mid-August."

Seth took a seat on the couch. "When does school start?"

"The third week of August."

"Hmm." He wanted Spud to move in soon. An idea began to form. "And once school starts, what were your plans for Nina while you're working?"

"It depends." Caroline lowered her body onto the chair diagonal from him. "If Fran's willing—and if I can afford it—I'd like Nina to go there after school. And I'm hoping Fran would watch her during school holidays."

"If she's not willing?"

"The daycare center is my only other option at this point." The words were quiet, matter-of-fact. "I'm praying Fran will be a good fit for Nina and that she's willing to babysit her. The sooner Spud can move in, the better."

"I want Spud here, too. I have an idea. What if after he passes his Canine Good Citizen test, he moves in? Instead of going with Nina to the daycare center, though, I'd come pick him up to spend the day with me."

"You'd do that?" He didn't miss the hint of incredulousness in her voice.

Heat flushed his face, and he shrugged one shoulder. "Yeah. Why not?"

"But it's out of your way. You're still living on the ranch."

"I drive to the boarding center every day to see the progress, anyhow." He hadn't realized how good it would feel to take this worry off her mind. "Let me know when you leave for work, and I'll make sure I get here early to pick him up."

"We leave at seven thirty. Should I come pick him up after work?"

"Nah, I'll drop him off for you."

Her attention directed to her lap where she'd folded her hands, then she met his gaze. "It seems you're always helping me and getting nothing in return."

"I get something." He hesitated. "I like helping you. I like spending time with Nina."

Speaking of the girl, she skipped into the living room. Liverwurst and Spud ambled behind her.

"What are we doing today, Mr. Hudson?"

"We're going to get Spud ready for his big test." Seth rose. "Let's start with the sit and stay commands. Are you up for it?"

"Yes!" She turned to Spud and motioned to him. "Sit."

Spud sat, looking expectantly to Nina.

"Okay, now tell him to stay," Seth said. "Then go to your room."

Nina giggled, then forced a serious tone. "Stay." She practically ran down the hall.

"Not excited at all, as you can tell." Caroline stood and picked up a notepad and pen from the coffee table.

Spud began walking toward the hall. Seth frowned. "He's supposed to stay." The panic on Caroline's face had him reassuring her. "Don't worry. He's been well-trained. Let's see what he does."

Seconds later, Nina's loud voice came to them. "No, Spud! You were supposed to stay in the living room." She sounded on the verge of tears.

The dog hustled down the hall straight to Caroline. His tail wagged, and he panted.

Seth didn't say a word, hoping she would recognize the dog's alert.

"It's Nina, isn't it, Spud?" She petted the dog's head and walked toward Nina's room. The girl met her in the hallway. Caroline bent and placed her hand on Nina's shoulder. "Let's check your reader."

Nina fumbled with the zipper of her waist pack, and Caroline took her by the hand, leading her to the couch, where she lifted her to take a seat. Then she took out the reader. The glucose levels were dropping.

Caroline glanced back at Seth. "I don't know how Spud knows, but he always does."

"We've trained him to know." Satisfaction surged. This was why he'd devoted all those years to training service dogs. To help people. Spud sat on the floor next to Nina with his chin resting on her legs, and Caroline's eyes glistened with appreciation.

"Caroline, you did good. You recognized he was alerting you, and you didn't get upset or mad that he broke out of the stay command."

"At first, I thought he wasn't obeying Nina." Caroline nodded. "But I could hear your voice in my head—'all the commands go out the window if he senses a glucose issue.' I'll be right back with some juice."

He glanced at Nina. "How are you feeling? You know Spud wasn't disobeying you, right? He could tell your glucose was low."

"What if he doesn't pass the test?" Her little voice warbled.

"You don't have to worry about that. He's going to pass. If he doesn't this Friday, he will next week. Spud's a smart dog. And you've been working hard at training him."

Nina's eyes filled with tears. "I'm scared he won't live here. I love him."

"If I didn't think he could be your dog, I would have told you way back when we started working with him," Seth explained, hating to see her upset. "It's never been a matter of if. It's always been a matter of when."

"But Spud didn't stay, and I told him to."

Caroline brought the juice to her. "Spud did what he's trained to do. You're too important for him to stay in the living room and obey you when he can tell you're having a glucose problem."

"Do I *have* to wear my reader after he lives here?" She stared up at her mother. Seth bristled. Had Caroline told her she wouldn't have to use the CGM?

"Yes. You always have to wear it. Always." Fear added unnecessary force to her words. "I want to hear you say it."

Nina slumped. "I always have to wear it."

"Good. We don't want Mr. Hudson thinking you're irresponsible. Spud will help you, but you still have to do your part. Insulin shots, checking the reader, eating properly."

"I don't want to be sick no more!" Nina ran to her room.

"Nina!" Caroline's face flushed red. She turned to him. "I'm sorry she was rude."

"Let's give her some space," Seth said quietly. "She wasn't rude. She's upset. It's okay."

"It's not okay." Caroline glared at him. "She knows better than to mouth off."

He was taken aback. What did he expect? He'd been thinking of Caroline as more than a friend while she clearly viewed him as the man training her daughter's dog.

She was the mom. He was some guy who should know his place.

Mission accomplished. He knew his place. And it was temporary. He didn't need her to spell it out for him again.

He'd been growing too close to her. And it had to stop before she broke his heart.

Chapter Nine

"He's got his paper!" Nina waved the Canine Good Citizen certificate in Seth's face Friday night.

Caroline sighed as she descended the back porch steps of her house. She'd just said goodbye to her dad. He'd helped Seth with the testing but had to leave to check on his older buddy, Darren, who'd been having some health problems. Her father had agreed to watch Nina the following Saturday while Caroline attended the training in Cheyenne. Unfortunately, her boss had been unwilling to reschedule it, but she'd talked him out of her having to stay overnight. At least she could count on her dad to babysit, although she had a lot of misgivings about being gone for so many hours.

She wished she could leave Nina with someone else. While she had no doubt her father loved her little girl, she wasn't sure he'd be on top of her diabetes care for ten hours straight. She had a week to get him up to speed before the training.

"You did a good job." Seth caught Nina up in his arms and held her on his hip. "Spud knows to obey you."

"I love Spuddy." Nina wrapped her arms around Seth's neck and planted a kiss on his cheek. "I love you, too, Mr. Hudson."

Caroline's step faltered on the grass. The words sliced through her heart.

Nina loved Seth.

Of course she did. He'd been so kind to her. Spent nearly every evening with them. How could Nina *not* love the man?

She paused to get her equilibrium back. She should be happy they got along so well, but part of her resented it.

Caroline had been the one to change every diaper, fret over each developmental milestone, take her to doctor after doctor before the diabetes diagnosis. She still woke up a few times each night, tiptoeing into her room to make sure her daughter was breathing. And, more often than not, Nina got lippy with her when she disciplined her or reminded her to check the reader.

It wasn't fair.

Seth had been distant with her since Monday, when Nina had had her outburst. Caroline wished he wouldn't second-guess her parenting. She already had enough doubts about her mothering skills as it was.

"I wish you were my daddy." With the certificate clutched in her hand, Nina stared into Seth's eyes. Those words were even more of a sucker punch to Caroline than her declaration of love. She couldn't move an inch if she tried.

"I think you're pretty special, Nina." His voice sounded raspy, and he set the girl back on her feet. "Now, let's celebrate. Sonny cooked up a good meal for us back at the ranch."

"I already ate." Nina stared at the certificate once more. "Can I see the ponies?"

"We can probably see a horse or two." Seth glanced at Caroline, and she forced a smile on her face. "Are you ready to go? We can take my truck."

"I'll drive separately. That way you don't have to drive us home later."

A shadow clouded his eyes, but he nodded. Then he called Liverwurst and Spud. "I'll see you over there."

"Can Spud stay with me?" Nina asked.

Seth waited for Caroline's response.

"No, he'll stay with Mr. Hudson. We're leaving in two minutes, anyhow." Caroline tried not to be short. "We'll see him at the ranch."

"But Mommy—"

"Stop, Nina," Caroline snapped. "I said no."

The girl pouted as she trudged up the steps.

Caroline waited for Seth to tell her she was wrong—again—and that the dog could go with them, but he simply adjusted his cowboy hat and led the dogs up the porch and through the sliding door without a word.

His silence was almost worse than him second-guessing her. She inhaled deeply. Being a mom wasn't always fun. She had to make rules. It wasn't all giggles and games for her.

Was it ever giggles and games for her?

Maybe she needed to loosen up. But if she did, Nina would think it was okay to be disrespectful. She couldn't win.

The pressure against her temples intensified, and she headed inside. She'd better get this supper at the ranch over with. Then Seth's family could meet the awful person who'd hurt him so cruelly years ago.

Maybe she wasn't being fair. They might not hate her. Meena had been kind at church.

After taking an ibuprofen for her headache, Caroline quickly packed a backpack with essentials for Nina. What was the temperature supposed to be later? She'd better grab sweatshirts for them in case it got cold. What about insulin? Did Nina need a shot now?

Nina was sitting on her bed with a stuffed bunny in her lap. Caroline opened the closet and pulled a zip-up hoodie off a hanger.

"Mommy, can Mr. Hudson be my daddy?" Nina hugged the bunny with a pensive air.

How could she possibly answer that?

"No." The answer wouldn't suffice, but she didn't know what else to say.

"Because I already have a daddy?" Nina's big, innocent eyes held hope, and Caroline's spirits sank even lower than she thought possible.

Was now the time to have this conversation? She didn't think so. They needed to drive to Hudson Ranch. And it wouldn't be fair for her to share such big news right before meeting Seth's family. Nina would need time to process it. They both would.

"No, that's not why."

"Is my daddy coming back?"

She focused on folding the hoodie, hating the emotions the words brought up. The backs of her eyes burned from the pressure. She was surprised she didn't burst into tears right then and there.

"No, he's not coming back. It's just us, kiddo." She turned to Nina and tried to reassure her with a smile, but she could feel her lips wobbling.

"Then Mr. Hudson *could* be my daddy."

Willing the emotions away, she raised her chin. "We need to leave. We'll talk about this another time, okay? Now, what does your reader say?"

Her disappointment was written all over her face. As Nina took out the reader and held it up for Caroline, she thought about how Seth and her dad had both advised her to tell Nina sooner rather than later.

She dreaded having the adoption talk with Nina. Didn't know how to explain the whys of it to the girl. Plus, if she was being really honest with herself, she worried it would harm her relationship with Nina, and lately, they already had enough strain between them.

What if the girl wanted her "real" mommy? Caroline had signed paperwork to keep the birth mother's identity a secret. She was legally obligated to withhold the information from Nina. As for the father? She'd never been told his name.

The pressure in her head increased. Tonight was supposed

to be special. Spud had passed his tests, and Seth was finally introducing her to his family. But it didn't feel special. It felt hard and stressful. Caroline wished she could go to bed and pretend everything was fine.

Nothing had been fine since the day her mother died.

She blinked twice. She'd never thought that before.

"See?" Nina said. "It's not beeping."

"Looks good. Why don't you wait for me in the living room?"

No matter how hard she tried to be as great a mom to Nina as her mom had been to her, she couldn't measure up. She'd never be able to fill those shoes. How she wished her mother could be here to offer guidance and support. It had been so hard not having her mom all these years.

Caroline headed to the bathroom to freshen up, then went to her own closet for a cardigan. Her gaze landed on the Bible on her nightstand shelf. God had gotten her through the past twelve years. She could count on Him.

"Mommy, let's go!" Nina called from the living room.

Caroline double-checked the backpack one more time before herding Nina outside. She opened the minivan door for her and helped strap her into the booster seat.

"When we get there, I need you to remember your manners. You're going to meet some of Mr. Hudson's family."

"He has a family?" Her stricken face forced Caroline to speak in a gentler tone.

"He has a brother and a sister. And some cousins."

"Oh." Nina looked thoughtful. "I want a brother or sister."

Of course she did. Another thing Caroline couldn't give her anytime soon. Today kept getting better and better. She kissed Nina's forehead. "I can't give you one of those, but I can give you a dog."

"I love Spud."

"I know you do, sweetie."

Caroline shut the door and settled into the driver's seat. She put on instrumental music and drove through town, thankful for Nina's silence. Ready or not, Caroline was about to meet Seth's family. At best, she figured it would be an uncomfortable evening. At worst? They'd disapprove of her.

Fun times. She should have backed out of going when she had the chance.

"I need you guys to behave." Seth addressed the squad. They were standing in a semicircle before him in the lodge's large dining room. He'd exceeded the speed limit to get there in time to prep his family before Caroline arrived. What if they all resented her because of how she'd treated him years ago? Would they make her feel unwelcome? He didn't want tonight to be awkward. He already had a lot of doubts about anything more than friendship with Caroline, but the squad didn't need to know that.

"What do you think we're going to do? Pick our noses in front of her?" Brody scoffed, shaking his head.

"Yeah, Seth, lighten up." Meena gave him an exaggerated eye roll. "I've spoken to her after church. She's nice. And Nina's a cutie."

Nina was a cutie. Seth wiped his sweaty palms down the sides of his jeans.

"Why are you so nervous?" Cooper seemed confused. "Get a grip."

"I'm not." Probably shouldn't have barked out the words. The adrenaline rushing through his veins made him jumpy. "I just want tonight to go smoothly."

"Why is it so important to you?" Hayden skewered him with eyes that saw too much. "You're into her again, aren't you?"

He didn't bother answering. Couldn't deny he had more than friendly feelings for Caroline. She didn't seem to be falling for him, which was good. He'd only get hurt if he gave her his heart. "Nina is excited about Spud."

"I'm looking forward to meeting Nina," Lillian said, holding Jonah. "She's probably thrilled to be getting a dog."

"She is." Seth flashed Lillian a smile. "She's great at handling Spud." Speaking of…both dogs had zoomed to the kitchen to find Butch. The three of them were probably lingering to catch a scrap while Sonny cooked.

Brody lifted his hands. "We will all treat Caroline and Nina as welcome guests, because they are. You don't have to worry, okay?"

The words eased some of his tension. The squad dispersed to the living room, but Meena stayed behind. "You like her, huh?"

"Nina? Of course." He knew who Meena was talking about, but he wasn't ready to go there.

"And her mom. It's okay, you know. People change. I hope you two can work things out."

People did change, but had Caroline? He wasn't sure. She'd been wound up tighter than a spool of fencing wire lately, and she'd made it abundantly clear he had no right to chime in about anything related to Nina's upbringing.

"Thanks, Meena." He meant it. His cousin tended to see the best in people. "I owe you for all the design work you did for the center."

"I love doing that. You don't owe me anything."

A knock on the front door propelled him into motion. In no time at all, he was introducing Caroline and Nina to the squad. Brody grinned and brought her in for a brief hug. Hayden gave her a nod. Cooper asked where she was living, and Spud trotted straight to Nina, who giggled and petted him.

"I hear Spud passed his tests today." Lillian handed Brody the baby and bent to speak to the girl.

"Yes, and he's going to live with me soon. He gets to sleep in my bedroom." Her shoulders crept up to her ears as she smiled. "Mommy said he gets a special bed."

"I like the sound of that. He's going to be so happy living

with you." Lillian straightened and held out her hand to Nina. "Want to go to the dining room with me? We're about ready to eat."

"I'm going to be happy living with him, too." Nina slipped her hand in Lillian's. "I'm going to read him books and scratch his belly and..."

Seth met Caroline's gaze as the two walked away. She seemed distracted. Worried. Was it because of him? Or meeting his family? Or the fact he'd barely spoken to her after her outburst on Monday? Maybe he should have told her flat out she'd hurt his feelings, that he'd felt dismissed.

Everyone headed to the dining room. After saying a table prayer, they passed around platters of burgers, French fries and pasta salad. Seth sat next to Caroline, and Nina was on her other side.

"Would you like anything to eat?" Caroline asked her.

"No, thank you."

Seth remembered Caroline saying she'd given Nina a light meal before testing Spud. Waiting to eat with his family this late would have thrown off her blood sugar.

"Do you like working for the law firm, Caroline?" Meena asked as she squirted ketchup next to her fries.

"Yes, it's interesting. I answer phones, take care of administrative work, and I've been typing notes for cases—that sort of thing."

"I'm in awe. My brain is always flitting from one thing to the next. Sitting still at a desk kills me."

Caroline smiled. "Seth tells me you're an interior designer."

"Well, kind of. I do online consulting for a large design firm. I really want to do more hands-on work."

While they talked about Meena's job, Seth ate his burger. Hayden and Brody were discussing how many calves they were expecting. Cooper had asked Sonny about the small garden he'd planted behind his house on the ranch. And Lillian was listening to Meena and Caroline, making comments here and there.

So far, so good.

"When does Spud get to live with you guys?" Meena asked Caroline.

Caroline cast a sideways glance his way. "It depends on Seth."

He'd been planning on telling her tonight. He might as well do it now. "If it's okay with you, I can bring him and all his stuff over tomorrow."

"Really?" Her face glowed as she blinked.

"He's ready. You're ready. I don't see the point in waiting." Seth then addressed Meena. "Spud will be hanging out with me while Caroline is at work."

Spud started wagging his tail and nudging Caroline.

Meena laughed. "Looks like he's excited about it, too."

"No, he senses something's wrong." Caroline shifted in her chair to address Nina. "Can you get the reader out for me?"

Nina nodded and unzipped her pack. Caroline glanced at Seth. "Normal."

Every time Spud alerted Caroline, the CGM would beep within a minute or two.

"Want to wait and see what happens?" Seth asked her. He wasn't surprised when she shook her head.

"Spud knows." Then she turned to Nina. "Why don't you get a candy ready, and we'll see what the reader says."

The girl nodded and fished in her elastic pouch for it while Caroline praised the dog. She unwrapped a candy right as the monitor began to beep. Caroline checked the reader—low, as she'd suspected, then pressed it and the beeping stopped.

Crisis averted. Seth couldn't have been prouder of Spud and how Caroline and Nina responded. If he'd needed another reason to justify having Spud live with them, he'd just gotten it.

"Wow." Meena exchanged a wide-eyed look with Lillian. "The dog really knows when she's having issues, doesn't he?"

"That was awesome." Cooper grinned.

"How did you know Spud wasn't just looking for attention?" Hayden asked.

Caroline flushed. "Seth taught me to recognize the signs. That's how the dog alerts me."

"What if Nina was in another room?" Brody's serious expression didn't seem to faze her.

"He'd come find me." Caroline turned her attention to Nina. "Feeling okay?"

She nodded shyly, then tugged on her mother's short sleeve. Caroline leaned down, and Nina whispered loudly, "When can I see the ponies?"

Brody let out a hearty chuckle. Seth couldn't help but smile, too.

"You like horses?" Brody winked at her.

"Yes."

"Hayden, you think we have some horses to show her?"

"We should be able to come up with a few." Was Hayden smiling? Seth rarely saw his brother relaxed and happy.

"Let everyone finish eating first, Nina," Caroline said. "And have another candy."

"Okay, Mommy."

The rest of the meal was full of easy conversation and laughter. It should have pleased Seth, but as everyone took their plates into the kitchen, he hung back. He could easily picture Caroline and Nina having many meals at the lodge in the future. But who was to say Caroline would want to come back? She'd given him no indication she had any interest in spending time with him after the training was over. And he couldn't see himself in a relationship with her if she wouldn't allow him to share his opinion on how to raise Nina.

Maybe introducing her to the squad had been a mistake.

Clearly, they all liked her. And he liked her, too. But he couldn't shake the idea that she was going to hurt him again. He didn't know how or when, but at some point, she'd accuse him of something awful, and he'd be right back to eighteen. Brokenhearted. And alone.

She could get used to hanging out with Seth's family. Caroline leaned against a fence post facing the green pasture while Seth boosted Nina to pet a quarter horse that had approached. Its nostrils quavered as Nina ran her hand down the white diamond on its forehead. Spud and Liverwurst were playing with each other nearby in the grass, and the sky blazed bright orange as the sun began to descend. What would it be like to be one of the Hudsons? Family suppers, teasing, laughter. All felt as far away to her as the moon barely visible in the sky.

"He's not as soft as Spuddy." Nina turned to look at Seth. "He likes me, doesn't he?"

"He sure does."

"What's his name?"

"Tango. He's Hayden's horse." Seth pointed beyond Caroline to where his brother stood near the gate. The two of them shared similar builds, but Seth was slightly shorter. Brody and Cooper stood on the other side of Seth. Meena had excused herself after supper to take a call, and Lillian had said she'd join them outside but needed to change Jonah first.

"Hey, Nina, here comes Shaggy." Brody hitched his chin to the palomino headed his way. "Best horse on the ranch."

"Says you," Hayden said loudly.

"You know I'm right." Shaggy went straight to Brody, who spoke sweet nothings to the horse as he stroked its neck. Then Brody turned to Nina. "Want to feed him a carrot?"

Nina's star-struck expression said it all, and Caroline suppressed a laugh. Her girl loved animals. She'd be jabbering on about it for days. Not that she minded. It felt good for them to have a night like this.

Brody handed Nina the carrot and told her how to hold it. Seth kept Nina on his hip as she held out the carrot. She shrieked and laughed as the horse's large teeth flashed. Soon the carrot disappeared amid loud crunching.

"Caroline, would you mind taking Jonah for me for a second?" Lillian had arrived and held out the baby to her. Caroline was startled, but she gladly took the chunky baby in her arms. His big drooly smile warmed her heart. How she missed holding a baby.

"You're pretty handsome there, huh, Jonah?" She adjusted his bucket hat. He bounced in her arms.

"Sorry, he gets excited being out here." Lillian finished adjusting the baby carrier. "I can take him back. The strap was killing me."

"I don't mind holding him. How old is he?"

"Eleven months. He turns one at the end of August." The ends of her shoulder-length black hair flickered in the breeze.

"I take it he isn't walking yet." She lightly bounced him, smiling at his chubby cheeks.

"Not on his own, but the way he cruises around the furniture tells me it won't be long."

Caroline chuckled. "He'll keep you busy. I remember how hard it was to keep Nina from running away from me when we were out and about."

Lillian winced. "Tell me that phase doesn't last long."

"It doesn't. Nina was great about holding my hand by the time she turned two."

"Two, huh? When did she start talking?"

"She was stringing together sentences by eighteen months, but I was told she talked early."

They chatted about toddler development, and several minutes later, Nina pulled on the hem of her shirt. "Can I see the baby, Mommy?"

Caroline glanced at Lillian for approval, and she nodded. Caroline bent, resting one knee on the ground, and kept a firm grip on the baby. "This is Jonah."

"Hi, Jonah," Nina said, touching his hand. He reached for her face, and she laughed. "You can't have my cheeks, mister." She proceeded to play peekaboo with him until he began to squirm.

"I think it's time he goes back to his mommy." She handed him to Lillian. "Thank you. I've missed holding a baby."

"Mommy, we should get a baby just like Jonah!" Nina slipped her hand in hers, and Caroline wanted to cherish the moment, but the words gave her heartburn.

Lillian smiled. "If only it were that easy."

Caroline wasn't sure how to respond, but Brody saved the day.

"What do you say we have a bonfire?" Brody took Jonah from Lillian and planted kisses all over his cheeks. He squealed in delight.

"Sounds good to me." Hayden touched the rim of his cowboy hat.

"Want to stay?" Seth had come over to stand next to Caroline. It was on the tip of her tongue to say they had to go home, but she glanced at Nina, whose mouth was open midyawn. Obviously, she should take Nina home and tuck her in bed. It had been a long, exciting day. But they'd been having fun, too. Would another hour be so bad?

She thought of how Seth and his family treated Nina, always asking her what she wanted. Maybe she should do the same.

"Would you like to stay for the fire, Nina?" Caroline asked. Why did the question make her anxious?

"Yes! I want to!" She hopped up and down.

"We'll stay for a while, but when I say it's time to leave, I don't want any arguing."

"Thank you!" Nina threw her arms around her waist and hugged her.

Caroline rubbed her back, then straightened and checked her phone. "It's almost time for your insulin."

"Come on, I'll go back to the lodge with you," Seth said before glancing back. "That's assuming you guys can handle getting the fire started without me."

Hayden guffawed. "Us? You couldn't start one without our help. We taught you everything you know about proper log placement."

"We'll be back in a few." Seth kept his hand at the small of Caroline's back, and a thrill went down her spine. "Want a piggyback ride, Nina?"

Her daughter did not have to be asked twice. Soon, Nina was perched on his shoulders with her bare legs and sneakers dangling. Caroline and Seth walked in easy silence down the lane.

"I can see why you moved back." She took in the trees on either side of the lane. "It's peaceful here. And your family is great."

"It is peaceful. And most of the time, my family's great." He smiled at her. She liked seeing him like this. Content. Relaxed. Happy.

"It was nice of you to invite us."

"I wanted you to meet everyone and for them to meet you."

She wanted to dissect that statement, but it would only give her false hope. She and Seth didn't have a future together, no matter how much her heart tried to tell her otherwise. He'd tire of her constant worrying and overthinking. And she wasn't sure about his second-guessing her parenting style.

"I like the baby," Nina said. "And the ponies. And the grown-up girls and boys."

"So, basically everyone?" Caroline grinned up at her.

She yawned again and wrapped her hands under Seth's chin. "I love them all," she said dreamily.

That was the problem. Nina did love them all, and Caroline found it easy to like them, too. But Seth would get tired of her and push her away.

Though Seth hadn't tired of her yet, and he knew exactly how her personality worked.

Was she really afraid of him pushing her away, getting tired of her controlling personality, second-guessing her parenting choices? Or was something else preventing her from getting close? Her mind flashed to the day her mother died. The phone call that had upended her world.

Panic hit her pulse, and she forced the memory out of her mind. She wouldn't think about it. Not here. Not now.

She wasn't sure she had anything to offer in a relationship, and she didn't have the energy for one, anyhow. But Seth tempted her. Oh, how he tempted her. If she fell in love, she'd lose him. She couldn't handle another loss.

"Mr. Hudson, I get to spend the whole day with my grandpa on Saturday." Nina sounded excited.

"Oh yeah?" He gave Caroline a curious look. "Tomorrow?"

"No, a week from tomorrow." The reminder triggered her anxiety. She did *not* want to drive to Cheyenne, spend hours in training and then drive home. Being away from Nina for that long scared her. She had to go over Nina's routine again with her dad. She'd been explaining how important it was to stick to the menu she'd planned, how to administer the insulin shots and to call the instant he wasn't sure about something.

Ever since moving back, she'd repeatedly tried to show him how to text, but he always laughed and told her he didn't do that. He'd pat her hand and assure her he'd call her with any problems. But would he? His communication style could only be described as sporadic.

At least Spud would be with Nina.

Maybe she should have asked Seth to watch Nina. *No.* That

would be crossing a line. She'd already been depending on him for too much.

"Grandpa's silly." Nina giggled. "I love him."

"I take it you won't be there?" Seth asked Caroline.

"I have work training. Out of town." Caroline didn't elaborate. Couldn't. Not without feeling out of breath.

"I'd offer to help, but the office at the boarding center will be finished this week, and Coop and I are getting all the computer equipment set up next weekend."

"You've already done so much for us. Dad will be fine." Seth didn't need to know she had doubts. But his sharp glance told her he'd picked up on them. "I'll be going over the insulin schedule, how to check the reader—all of it. I'll bring Spud to his place this week to go over that aspect with him, too."

"Tell him I'll be at the center if he needs anything."

"But you're busy—"

"I'm not that busy. Besides, I doubt he'll call. It's just for backup."

Relief at his offer helped ease her nerves. "I'll tell him. Thank you."

Ten minutes later, after giving Nina her insulin shot, they joined his family around a fire pit near a semicircle of cabins down a side lane.

"What are all those little houses?" Nina pointed to the circle drive.

"See that cabin?" Seth asked Nina. "I live there. But soon I'm going to live near town."

"You live there?" she asked breathlessly.

"Yep, that cabin is mine. We each have our own."

"Ooh. I'd like to live in a little house like that."

"Are you cold, Nina?" Caroline asked.

"No."

Caroline and Seth settled in chairs, and Nina climbed up on his lap. The sky had grown dark, and the drop in temperature made her glad for the warmth of the fire. The crackles and pops of the fire accentuated the lively conversation among the cousins. She was content listening to them tease each other, but she also answered any questions they asked.

By the time an hour passed, Nina had fallen asleep.

Seth rose. “I’ll carry her to your car.” Caroline said goodbye to everyone and grabbed the backpack. They walked in silence as the stars above sparkled like gems in the sky. She wanted to thank him for the evening, for finishing Spud’s training, for all of it, but she didn’t know where to begin. When they reached her minivan, Seth carefully strapped Nina, still sleeping, into her booster seat, then shut the door and faced Caroline.

She shivered and rubbed her forearms. He put his arms around her, drawing her to him. “You’re cold.”

“No, I’m fine.” She made no effort to step out of his embrace as she inhaled his masculine cologne.

“You always say that—you’re fine.” His voice was tender. “Let me warm you up.”

She felt the rapid beat of his heart through his shirt. She shouldn’t be hugging him. She needed to be strong. To drive home. To keep doing what she’d been doing for years—everything. On her own.

And yet she couldn’t drum up the energy to leave. Being in his arms made her forget she needed to keep her life together all by herself, that she couldn’t trust anyone to meet her standards.

“Thanks, Seth, I needed that.”

“Needed what?”

“Tonight. Your family—they’re so welcoming and kind. And you—you’ve taken such a burden from me with Spud and by just being around you.”

He eased back slightly, and even in the darkness with only the lights from the sky, she could see the tenderness in his eyes, his attraction to her, the implicit offer that he’d help if she’d let him.

And then he lowered his mouth to hers, and she placed her hands on his chest, then over his shoulders, behind his neck. She matched his kiss, remembering when he'd kissed her that summer before her mom died.

This kiss held so much more than teenage dreams.

It held substance, longing and the admission that the past twelve years had been difficult for them both. And it made her want to sink in, claim him, surrender. Forever.

Seth broke away first, stepping back, raking his hand through his hair. "That probably wasn't smart."

Smart? No, it wasn't. And she always prided herself on doing the smart thing. "You're right. But maybe smart is overrated. This time." Then she got into the driver's side.

"I'll be over tomorrow with Spud and his supplies." He lifted a hand in goodbye, and she closed the door and started the minivan.

Seth was correct. The kiss hadn't been smart. She needed to use better judgment from now on. But that kiss…she'd tuck it in her heart. She wouldn't be forgetting about it anytime soon.

Chapter Ten

With the center close to being finished, Seth needed to start getting the word out about the facility. He'd been waiting to advertise until he was sure of the grand opening date. Yesterday, Hector had assured him everything would be done before Labor Day weekend.

Seth opened a large cardboard box and unpacked office chair parts. It had been over a week since the bonfire…and the kiss. A bag full of wheels fell out of the box. He set it aside. All week, he'd been picking up Spud in the morning before Caroline left for work and then dropping off the dog in the evening. A few times, she'd politely asked him to stay, and while he'd wanted to hang out the way they had before Spud passed his tests, Seth had declined. His feelings for Caroline confused him.

He'd been certain she felt more for him than just friends. But her comment about smart being overrated *this time* had implied it wouldn't be smart in the future. As much as he tried to tell himself he was overthinking it, he couldn't stop overanalyzing her reaction to his kiss. And Caroline's quiet thank-you each night for dropping off Spud wasn't helping. Something had changed between them after the bonfire, and he didn't like it.

He screwed the seat into the chair base and began attaching the arms. What was it about her he couldn't get off his mind? Why couldn't his heart take his word for it that she'd only hurt him?

Are you sure about that? You're pretending she's the same Caroline that she was at eighteen. Didn't she tell you you've taken some of her burdens from her? And you can't pretend spending time with her and Nina hasn't gotten you out of a rut. They're easy to be with. So why are you fighting it?

Caroline had a her-way-or-the-highway mentality when it came to Nina. And it wasn't like they were dating. But if they were, would she listen to him?

Maybe he'd better get his head back into launching this center—where it belonged. The squad had invested a large sum of money into this place, and he hadn't exactly been prioritizing it—he'd been training Spud and hanging out with Caroline and Nina.

After attaching the arms to the chair, he quickly popped the wheels into place and stepped back to make sure he hadn't missed any parts.

"Sorry I'm late." Cooper carried two takeout coffees as he entered the office. Liverwurst woke from his nap and wagged his tail. "Thought you might want some caffeine."

"You must have read my mind. Thanks." Seth took one of the cups.

"Smells like fresh paint. I like the color." Cooper's gaze went to the ceiling corner and slowly took in the rest of the room. "Meena was right about all the lighting in here and at the front desk area."

"Yeah, she knows her stuff." Seth took a tentative sip and winced. "Sit and Sip doesn't mess around with their coffee. This could melt steel."

Coop laughed. "I took my lid off all the way here. It helped."

"Want a quick tour?" Seth hitched his thumb to the door.

"Sure. A lot has changed since I was last here." They carried their coffees out to the main reception area, and Liverwurst sniffed his way around the front counter facing the entrance door. Below the counter, a row of cabinets had been installed.

"This way for the boarding rooms." Seth headed to the left.

"You mean suites." Cooper grinned. "Meena's corrected me more than once."

"She has an odd aversion to referring to them as a room, crate, kennel or cage." Seth chuckled, shaking his head. "So yeah, the overnight suites. I'm glad I decided on individual rooms instead of kennels. She was right about that, too. It's more comfortable for the dogs."

They stopped at the first suite. Partitions had been installed with four-foot-high paneling topped with Plexiglas windows.

"I went with textured epoxy floors for easy cleanup and so the dogs aren't slipping and sliding." Seth pointed to the floor.

"What are they going to sleep on?" Cooper stepped into the small area and gave it a thorough perusal.

"Each room will have a raised bed topped with a machine-washable cushion. Stainless steel bowls will go there." Seth pointed his boot to the front corner. "And we'll be able to get the dogs outside easily since the rooms have pass-through doors."

"I like it. This is great."

Seth answered Cooper's questions as they strolled to the end of the aisle and turned the corner to the indoor play areas.

"Whoa. The windows really made this bright." Three banks of windows had been installed along the wall.

"That's what we were going for."

"How will this be divided? You're planning to have a couple of play areas, right?"

"Yes. One for larger dogs, and one for smaller ones. Their temperament will play a factor, too."

"Did you order the play equipment?" Cooper paused to look out the window of one of the doors leading to the outdoor play area.

"I did. Most of it will be here next week. Some of it was on back order."

Cooper nodded, then turned to face him. "What happened to the grass?"

"I'm having turf installed." Seth joined him and stared out at the dirt. "Reduces mud and discourages digging."

"I never would have thought of that."

"The dogs deserve to be as comfortable as possible away from home, and I don't want to spend all my time cleaning mud dragged in from outside."

They made their way back to the office at the front of the building. Two oblong boxes leaned against the wall in the hallway.

"Give me a hand with these desks, will you?" Seth picked up one end, and Cooper got the other. They hauled each box into the office, and Seth sliced one of them open. "Shouldn't be too complicated."

"Famous last words."

They finished their coffees, then worked on assembling the first desk.

"How's Spud doing now that he's living with Nina?" Coop asked as he tightened a screw.

"Good. I can tell he misses her during the day. He gets excited when I drop him off every night."

"I noticed you've been getting home earlier now that he lives there."

"Yeah, well, his training is done." Seth didn't like coming home earlier. He missed his time with Caroline.

"I'm surprised."

"About what?"

Cooper set the screwdriver on the floor. "You and Caroline seemed to be getting along well at the ranch last weekend."

"We're friends." After the kiss, he might have qualified them as more than friends, but not now. Each day that passed, a little more distance grew between them. Probably because he'd put the distance there. Maybe he should have hung out with her a night or two.

"She's nice." Cooper wouldn't let it go.

"I know." He didn't mean to sound gruff. One of the table legs wasn't fitting correctly. He pushed it, and it still wasn't right.

"Seems to like you. Nina sure does."

"Yeah, so?"

"You live in Fairwood. She lives in Fairwood..." His lilting tone grated on Seth's nerves.

"What about it? You live in Fairwood, too."

"I'm not looking to date anyone."

Seth pounded the side of the leg and it clicked into place. Finally. "I'm not, either."

"I don't buy it."

"There's nothing to buy." His chest grew tight. He didn't want to talk about it.

"I get that she hurt you. But it was a long time ago, and she'd literally buried her mom a few hours before the dog died. You could give her a chance, you know." What Cooper was saying made sense. "Unless you're worried about the kid. It's a big responsibility. Diabetes."

"That doesn't bother me." He'd tear off his right arm for Nina.

"Then what does?" Cooper rolled the chair over and sat in it. It didn't collapse beneath his weight. At least Seth knew he'd put it together correctly.

"She doesn't trust me." Not with the things that mattered most. She'd ignored his advice to tell Nina about being adopted. She didn't want him to say a word about Nina's upbringing.

"Are you sure about that?"

She'd trusted him at the ranch. She'd admitted she'd needed him. But...she had trust issues a mile wide, and he wasn't sure why.

"Yeah, I am." Seth grabbed another table leg.

"She trusted you to train the dog."

"Yeah, and she'll probably blame me the second anything goes wrong."

Cooper pulled a doubting face. "You think?"

Seth nodded. It gave him no pleasure to admit that. But he wasn't playing pretend this time. He'd gone into training Spud with his eyes wide-open. As soon as Caroline found a babysitter or school started—whichever came first—he'd have no reason to see her.

He should be glad. But the disappointment slithering through him assured him he'd done a bad job of protecting his heart. He should have set more limits. Shouldn't have spent so much time with her and Nina.

He'd grown too close to them both.

His cell phone rang. "Hello?"

"Seth. Good. You answered." Ken Bright sounded breathless. If he remembered correctly, Caroline was out of town for work training.

"What's wrong? Is it Nina?"

"No, she's fine. It's my buddy Darren. He called me sounding funny, and I heard a thunk, and I yelled his name, but he didn't answer. I called 9-1-1, but they can't get out to his place for half an hour. I'm running over there right now. The problem is I'm watching Nina—and I don't want to frighten her."

"I'm at the center. Where does Darren live?"

Ken rattled off an address nearby.

"Drop Nina and Spud off here. I'll take care of them while you check on your friend."

"I was hoping you'd say that. Be there in five." The line went dead.

Seth explained what was going on to Cooper, and the two of them finished putting together the first desk. Then they, along with Liverwurst, headed outside the entrance to watch for Ken.

His vehicle pulled into the drive, and soon, Nina was running to Seth, launching herself into his arms. Spud ambled up to them. Ken held out her backpack, and Cooper took it from him.

"Caroline left instructions and insulin and snacks and everything in there." Ken's face looked ashen.

"Go. I know what to do." Seth clapped his hand on the man's shoulder. "Call me when you know something."

"Will do." He nodded, turning back to the open door of the driver's side.

"Oh, wait, should I call Caroline?" He held Nina on his hip. Cooper stood next to him, and Spud greeted Liverwurst with a wagging tail.

"Don't worry about it. I'll let her know. She's in training all day. Doesn't want to be disturbed. Won't be home until eight or nine." The man slipped into the driver's seat, shut the door and drove off.

Seth set Nina on her feet. "When was the last time you ate?"

"Grandpa gave me breakfast, but it was a long time ago." Her hair had been pulled into two pigtails. "I'm hungry."

He checked his phone. Almost lunchtime. "Let's go to Tootsie's Diner and have some lunch."

"I need a shot first," she said in a matter-of-fact tone.

"Right." Seth motioned for Cooper to hand him the backpack. "We'd better go in the house and figure this out. Coop, you joining us?"

"I'll let you two figure out the shot situation. But lunch at Tootsie's?" Cooper grinned. "I'm in."

"Will you get Spud's service dog vest on him?" Seth tossed Coop the vest. "I'll crate Liverwurst in the center before we leave."

"Sure thing." Cooper crouched in front of Spud. "Let's get this on you, big guy."

Seth carried Nina to the house and unlocked the front door. "Probably should wash our hands first."

"Mommy and Ms. Briana always wash their hands first."

"Who's Ms. Briana?" He gave her a boost at the kitchen sink, and she giggled as the water sprayed.

"She's my daycare teacher. Where's the soap?" Her eyebrows drew together.

"I don't have any yet. Um, no towels, either. Rub your hands really good under the water. I'll grab some paper towels and be right back." He turned off the faucet and set her on her feet. Then he crossed to the other counter and ripped several paper towels from a roll. When her hands were dry, he rummaged through the backpack and found laminated instructions on administering insulin. Caroline had laid it out in an easy-to-understand way. He sure was glad she'd planned ahead. He found one of the insulin pens and a needle.

"Where do you usually get the shots?" Now that he was responsible for giving her the insulin, he didn't want to hurt her.

"Mommy changes spots so I don't get sore." She pointed to her left thigh. "I can do it, Mr. Hudson."

"It doesn't say on this sheet that you're allowed to give yourself the shot." He frowned as he read it carefully. "I'd better do it."

"I need a wipey!" She pointed to the square packets in a baggie. Seth pulled one out, opened it and gave her the wipe. She pushed up the hem of her shorts and wiped a spot on her leg. "The needle doesn't go in yet. You have to push the air out." Her cheerful expression was doing a number on his heart. How could a kid be so mature about this?

"Why don't you show me?" He handed her the pen. Caroline's instructions mentioned removing air bubbles, but he figured Nina had seen it enough to know what needed doing.

"See? And turn to the two." With her tongue sticking out, she adjusted the pen, then gave it to Seth, who took a needle and peeled off the tab. "I watch Mommy every day. I know how."

"You're really smart, Nina, you know that?"

"I'm a big girl." She beamed at him as he attached the needle to the end of the pen. "It has to point to the sky first." After he shifted the pen so the needle was upright, she told him to tap the pen. "Now give it a pushy until a drop comes out."

He did. She pointed to her tiny leg, and he gulped. Didn't think of himself as a wuss, but he didn't want to cause the girl any pain. "Right here?"

She pinched the skin, and when he had the shot close, she helped him guide it. As he pressed the plunger, she counted, "One, two, three..."

Seth watched in amazement as she counted to ten. Then he removed the shot.

"All done! Can we eat now?"

"Yes, we can." He set the used pen on the counter to get rid of later. Then he bent to her level. "But first, I want to tell you how proud I am of you."

"Why?" She reached for his hand, and they walked to the front door.

"Because you helped me and didn't complain. I've never given anyone an insulin shot before."

"Mommy says they help me so I can learn and play. I feel yucky if I don't have them. Last year I had to go the hospital, and I don't want to go there again."

His chest tightened as he held the door open and waited until she was on the porch before locking it.

"The hospital, huh? That must have been scary."

"Mommy was with me. She got me my stuffed bunny. And then the doctor gave us the reader, and I haven't gone to the hospital since."

"Your mommy loves you very much. She's pretty smart."

"I know. I have the best mommy in the whole world!"

Seth privately agreed. Caroline had been taking care of this child since birth. Instead of judging her for not listening to his thoughts about Nina, he should be supporting her.

He admired her more and more. And he was tired of pretending he didn't have feelings for her. He did. They were real, and they ran deep. Maybe it was time to tell her some of the things on his mind. If she wasn't interested, at least he'd know.

But he was pretty sure she *was* interested. He was ready to take a chance at more—if he could get the guts to tell her.

She'd survived the entire day of training. Caroline waved goodbye to the people she'd sat with and got into her car. Took a moment to slow her breathing. She couldn't wait to get home and wrap Nina in her arms and kiss the top of her head. The training had been interesting, and she'd enjoyed meeting new people. She was already thinking of ways she could implement the things she learned. At times she'd become so engrossed in the information, she'd completely forgotten about her dad and Nina.

Unfortunately, this morning she'd gotten a sensor signal loss alert from the CGM app, so she didn't know if Nina had dealt with any blood sugar problems. She'd checked her phone off and on all day for missed calls, and she'd tried to call her father during both breaks. The fact he hadn't picked up wasn't a surprise—he often had the volume turned down. And his voicemail had been full—as usual—so she couldn't leave a message.

Was it good or bad that she hadn't heard from her dad?

Probably good. After starting the car, she backed out of the spot and began the long drive home. Maybe she should give him a quick call and make sure everything was okay.

Using the Bluetooth, she dialed his number. It rang and rang.

His lack of response usually produced a fleeting, mild annoyance in her, but today? As she headed out of town, her hackles rose. Why couldn't he keep his phone close and the volume up? He knew how important it was for her to keep track of Nina's health. And she'd made it clear it was difficult to leave her baby for so long.

She gripped the steering wheel as her nerves sizzled. When

she got home, she'd just have to explain it again—she needed her father to be better about answering the phone when Nina was in his care.

The city streets faded, and soon rolling prairies came into view. At least there wasn't any traffic. Hopefully, she'd be home by eight. It would give her plenty of time to hear all about Nina's day and slip Spud an extra treat for watching over her girl.

After turning on the radio, she flipped the channel to a contemporary Christian station. Her thoughts went to Seth. All week they'd tiptoed around each other. Each morning when he picked up Spud, her tongue tied itself into knots, and when he dropped off the dog after work, all she wanted to do was beg him to come in and stay a while. But simultaneously her mind was fixated on juggling quality time with Nina and doing all the nightly chores. She didn't understand why she'd found it easy to be with him before Spud was certified. Now her emotions were bouncing all over the place.

The kiss.

She'd thought about Seth's kiss roughly seventy-two thousand times this past week. What surprised her wasn't the fact that he'd kissed her but that it had felt so right. Having his arms around her and his lips pressed to hers had crumbled defenses she'd had in place for years.

Her ex-boyfriend's voice tripped through her mind. *It's always your way or the highway.*

But Seth didn't seem to view her like that. He'd been around her enough to see how she handled Nina's disease—with careful planning and checklists galore. It hadn't scared him off.

Could he be the safe spot she'd been longing for?

The highway divided the prairie for miles. Nothing could hide out there if it tried. And it reminded her of her heart. She kept trying to hide her feelings, but Seth was making it impossible.

He'd spoken his mind about important things, like wanting her to tell Nina she was adopted. He was patient with her daughter and hadn't disrespected Caroline's wishes. If she took a chance and told him how she felt about him, would he respect her decisions when it came to Nina?

As the miles flew by, the uneasiness in her gut grew. Her dad should have seen her missed calls. Why hadn't he called her back?

Today wasn't the right day to have the sensor signal lost on her phone. What if Nina had passed out from a low-blood-sugar episode and her dad missed it? What if he accidentally left Spud outside and the dog couldn't alert him? What if he'd been playing proud grandpa and had given her ice cream or candy? What if he'd forgotten to give her the insulin? What if something had happened to her dad?

She glanced at her phone again. No notifications. The uneasiness grew to full-blown worry.

Every Sunday the pastor urged the congregation to take their problems to the Lord. Maybe she should pray. And if she did, then what?

Prayers didn't always get answered the way she wanted. Until she saw Nina with her own eyes and held her in her arms, she didn't have the luxury of believing everything was fine.

By the time she pulled into her driveway, her anxiety levels had shot sky-high. She gathered her things and hurried up the front porch. Inside, the quiet stillness made the hair on her arms stand on end.

"Hello? Dad? Nina?" She went to the kitchen. A note in her dad's handwriting sat on the counter.

At the hospital. Call Seth.

Her heartbeat pounded in rapid bursts. At the hospital? What had happened? All she could picture was Nina hooked up to tubes and machines—like last year—and wondering where her mommy was.

Fumbling for her phone, she steadied it long enough to call Seth. He answered on the second ring.

"What happened?" She fought to keep her tone neutral as she prepared for the worst.

"What do you mean?"

"How is Nina? What hospital are you at?"

"Nina's fine." The sound of a cartoon in the background did nothing to allay her fears. "She's at the ranch with me. We're watching a cartoon."

"I'll be right there." She ended the call and raced back out to her minivan. As she drove to the ranch, she clenched her fingers around the wheel.

She never should have left Nina with her dad. And for her father not to call and tell her what was going on was completely unacceptable.

What *was* going on? Why was her daughter at Hudson Ranch?

Seth should have called—or at least texted—to tell her that he had her daughter. Obviously, neither Seth nor her dad had a clue how important Nina was to her. Caroline wouldn't make the mistake of trusting them with her baby girl again.

Chapter Eleven

"Your mom's on her way." As Seth packed Nina's backpack, apprehension seeped through him. Caroline had sounded strange on the phone. And then she'd hung up on him before he could ask her what she'd meant or tell her how the day had gone. He didn't like it.

He'd explain what happened when she arrived. If she'd waited, he'd have driven Nina and Spud to her place.

"Spud's tired." Nina was sprawled out on the sectional in the lodge with Spud on the floor beside her. She yawned.

"I think you might be tired, too."

"No, I'm not tired." She snuggled deeper, pulling a fuzzy pink throw up to her neck. Meena had brought it over earlier. Her eyelids closed.

Seth had enjoyed today more than he'd thought possible. After lunch at Tootsie's—he'd ordered a burger for himself, Nina had wanted the kid's chicken tender platter and Cooper had opted for the daily special—Seth had picked up Liverwurst from the center and taken the dogs and Nina back to the ranch. Lillian had brought Jonah over to the lodge for a while, and Nina had loved playing with the baby. Then Meena had stopped by on a work break and painted Nina's fingernails a shimmery pink shade.

He and Nina had managed the other insulin shots pretty well, and Spud had only alerted him twice to glucose dips.

All in all, it had been a great day. He'd gotten through caring for her fine without Caroline's help. It had given him a taste of what being Nina's daddy would look like, and the idea was growing on him more and more. He wanted to be there for Caroline—emotionally, physically, anything she needed. And he'd love nothing more than to help raise this precious little girl.

He zipped the backpack and set it in the hall near the front door. Until he'd kissed her, communicating with Caroline had been simple. Since then, not so much. Her tone on the phone kept eating away at him.

He shook his head. No need to read into things. Why make trouble where there wasn't any? When she got here, he'd tell her what happened, and they'd be back to normal.

His nerves ratcheted as the clock tick-tocked. Nina slept soundly, and Spud did, too. After what felt like an eternity, a sharp knock on the door made him jump. He strode over and opened it.

Caroline's brown eyes were wide with fear. She pushed past him. "Where is she?"

"Sleeping on the couch." His nerves flipped from nervous to defensive in an instant. "Don't wake her."

To her credit, she made her way to the couch in silence, gently placing her hand on Nina's hair and kissing her forehead. Then her shoulders straightened, and with a quick flick of her fingers, she gestured for him to follow her. They strode in silence down the hall and out on the front porch. He left the door cracked open to hear the CGM and for Spud to come find him.

She whirled to face him, and her expression took him back twelve years ago. To her farm after the funeral. He braced himself for her scream.

But she didn't scream. Instead, she leveled an angry, resigned glare his way.

"Why isn't my dad watching Nina?"

"Darren called him. He wasn't feeling well, and he collapsed while they were on the phone."

Her jaw shifted as she absorbed what he said. "Dad took him to the hospital?"

Seth nodded, his muscles tensing at the attitude pulsing from her.

"And he asked you to take care of Nina?"

"Yes. And he called an hour ago to let me know Darren would be there overnight. Ken's staying with him at the hospital since the guy has no family around."

She sucked in her cheeks, and her nostrils flared. "And neither of you thought to tell me this?"

"What do you mean?" Seth drew his eyebrows together. "Ken said he'd told you."

Her disgusted sniff and eye roll had him crossing his arms over his chest.

"I got home to a note. It said, 'At the hospital, call Seth.'"

"I thought he called you. He told me you were in training and not to disturb you."

"Disturb me?" Her voice rose. "Don't you think I'm disturbed enough thinking my child was taken to the hospital? And no one thought to tell me? Why on earth wouldn't you text me? Or better yet, call?"

"I told you why," he said quietly. It was happening again. She was accusing him of things he wasn't responsible for. "I thought you knew."

"You have no idea how scared I was to leave town today, and I had serious doubts about leaving Nina with my dad in the first place."

"I get that it's hard to leave Nina for a long time, but your dad is great with her. Can't you give him the benefit of the doubt?" Didn't she realize how unfair she was being? "He's raised hundreds of puppies. He's a responsible guy."

"So responsible he didn't bother letting me know he shoved

Nina into the first available arms he could find?" Her head began to do a weird shaking thing. "You should have texted me. You should have—"

"Stop it." He didn't recognize the strength in his own voice. "Your dad had an emergency, and I volunteered to take care of Nina. And I took care of her just fine."

"You don't even know how to give her insulin or when she needs it. You have no clue what she needs!" She was reaching a point of hysteria, and he couldn't drum up a sliver of sympathy for her.

"I figured it out." His insides were turning to stone. "You left step-by-step instructions even a child could understand. Give me some credit."

"Oh, yes, I'm overbearing because I left instructions. I'm a terrible mom for not wanting my daughter to die of low blood sugar."

"I didn't say that. I don't even know where you're coming up with this stuff." His blood began to simmer. "Do you know Nina actually showed *me* exactly how to give her the shots? She practically did it herself before supper while I supervised."

Caroline looked like she'd been slapped. She blinked rapidly. "She's too young. Practically a baby. And you let her give herself insulin?"

Her horrified tone stripped away the last of his patience.

"I forgot, Caroline," he said sarcastically, "you can't trust me. Never could. I killed your dog, after all. And I'm so dumb and irresponsible, I'd just let your daughter die on my watch. I wouldn't even realize it. Because no one—*no one*—could ever care as much as you do. Not about Lucy, not about Nina, not about anything."

"That's not fair." The words came out a hiss.

"You know what's not fair? Getting blamed for things I didn't do. Having you think the worst of me because you're so scared of losing someone, you'll lash out at anyone to keep them from getting close to you."

The blood drained from her face, but she didn't argue, didn't defend herself. Certainly didn't apologize.

"I thought we were friends, but friends don't think the worst of each other. I'm such a fool. I thought..." He looked her up and down with disdain. "I thought we had something, Caroline."

He pushed the door open and went inside. Swiped the backpack off the floor. Caroline followed him. He shoved it into her hands. "Here. Take your stuff and go. I'll get Nina."

With adrenaline surging, he stalked to the sectional and tenderly scooped up Nina, blanket and all. Spud got to his feet and followed him as he strode down the hall, past Caroline, down the porch steps to her minivan.

He waited for her to open the side door, and then he got Nina buckled. He smoothed the stray curl near the child's temple and stepped aside. Closed the door. Then he waited a beat. But Caroline didn't apologize.

"So this is how it's going to be?" Seth moved closer to her. And the one thing that still irked him refused to stay inside. "Do yourself a favor and tell Nina the truth soon. You think she's a helpless baby, but she's not. She's asking a lot of questions, and she deserves to know she's adopted."

"I'm her mother. I know what's best for her." Her cheekbones jutted beneath her skin.

"Yeah, well, I know you think you're mom of the century, but it's time you wake up and deal with it."

She pushed past him, got into the driver's seat and slammed the door. He didn't bother sticking around. He retreated to the porch as she drove away.

Treated like garbage again. Now he knew what Caroline really thought of him. The same as she'd thought the first goround. Incompetent. Untrustworthy.

His fantasy of being a husband and dad vanished like smoke spiraling into the sky.

Caroline Bright had broken his heart twice.

There wouldn't be a third time.

She hadn't realized she'd fallen in love with him. If she had to pinpoint the moment she'd known, it had been when he'd told her he thought they had something.

They did. They did have something. Or they had before tonight.

The drive home had exhausted her after an already long, draining day. Nina had woken briefly when Caroline pulled into their drive and drowsily told her all about her adventures—Mr. Hudson this, and Mr. Hudson that—until Caroline tucked her into bed and escaped to the living room.

She curled her legs beneath her on the couch. Smooth jazz music wasn't helping settle her nerves. Nothing would.

When Seth accused her of believing she was mom of the century, the words had hacked into her innermost being, leaving her bloodied and confused. She'd wanted to tell him she didn't think that at all. That she always felt unqualified to be a mother. Between the diabetes, sending Nina to daycare all day and not having a father for the girl, Caroline typically felt seventeen rungs below every other mother on the planet.

But it was the other thing he'd said that festered inside her. She didn't want to think about it. Didn't want to examine it. But it pressed against her chest. *You're so scared of losing someone, you'll lash out at anyone to keep them from getting close to you.*

She couldn't deny it. Hadn't realized that's what she'd been doing for twelve long years. But the truth couldn't be shoved back into the bag. It was out. And she didn't like it.

She should go to bed, try to rest. Today had taken everything out of her, and yet, she was too keyed up to sleep.

Seth didn't want to be friends anymore. No shock there.

She'd been stunned he'd given her a second chance to begin with. She was not surprised that she'd blown it.

Wasn't that her thing? Ruining their relationship with awful accusations? Assuming the worst about Seth because it was easier than trusting him?

He'd overlooked her flaws. He'd thought they'd had something. She'd thought the same. But she'd nuked any future with him after tonight.

Why hadn't she listened to him? Thanked him for watching Nina during an emergency? She should have asked how their day went and appreciated all he'd done to keep Nina safe and happy. But her fears had overridden common sense. Her overblown worries had worked her into a state that she couldn't have gotten out of if she'd tried.

Sometimes she hated herself.

Caroline stretched out her legs and stood. Crossed over to the side table where a framed photograph of Nina as a toddler stood. Then she gazed around the room. The same room she'd tidied in a hurry this morning before racing out the door after her dad had arrived to watch Nina.

Same room. Same old Caroline.

What would her mother have to say if she were here? How could Caroline possibly explain her actions to the woman?

Well, Mom, I was worried about Nina, and Dad didn't call me, and I flew into a frenzy and basically accused Seth—again—of negligence.

It had been so long since she'd heard her mother's voice, she couldn't remember what she sounded like. But she was pretty sure her mom's reply would have been full of disappointment. Her mother had always cautioned her to try to put the best construction on things. To believe the best in people instead of the worst.

I let you down, Mom. All I do is let everyone down.

She went to the kitchen and poured herself a glass of water.

Why couldn't she have seen the positive earlier? Why couldn't she give Seth—and her father, for that matter—the benefit of the doubt?

Well, to be fair, they weren't giving *her* the benefit of the doubt, either.

It irritated her that the two of them acted like she was hurting Nina by not telling her about being adopted. It wasn't any of their business. She'd tell the girl when the time was right.

And Seth *should* have known better than to take her dad's word for it about notifying her of the change in plans. Caroline shouldn't have to spell it out for them. The worst thing? She *had* spelled it out. Many times.

Why did they think it was okay for her to be left out of the loop? What if something had happened to Nina? What if they'd had to take her to the hospital? Would they have even called her?

The glass slipped from her hand and fell into the sink. It didn't break. She gripped the edge of the counter with both hands as her chin dropped.

She hadn't even begun to process the fact that Seth had basically allowed Nina to give herself the insulin shot. Anything could have gone wrong. They could have forgotten to remove the air bubble. Or not waited the full ten seconds before taking out the needle. Had they cleaned her skin first? Washed their hands?

A twitching sensation fluttered below her eye. She went back to the living room and curled up on the couch.

Seth had been right about one thing. Whatever they'd had was over. And it was all her fault.

Probably for the best. She'd known all along she'd drive him away. But she hadn't realized she'd feel so bad about it when it happened.

She didn't deserve Seth Hudson. And she never would.

Chapter Twelve

Seth quickly scanned the pews at church the next day. Caroline usually went to early service, but he didn't see her or Nina this morning. Just as well. He'd barely slept, and even if she did show up, last night they'd said all there was to say.

She wouldn't apologize to him. He knew that for certain. She hadn't twelve years ago, and she wouldn't now. So why was he looking for her? Didn't make sense.

He'd be better off erasing her from his mind. But that was easier said than done.

He slipped into the pew next to Meena and Cooper.

Meena's eyebrow rose to the ceiling. "Early service? You?"

"You look like you had a fight with a bear and the bear won." Cooper's face screwed into a grimace. "What happened?"

"Will you two shut it?" He was not in the mood for them today. Wasn't in the mood for anything. He wanted to forget the past two months had happened. How had he slipped back into a relationship with Caroline? Hadn't the first time she'd broken his heart been bad enough?

"Did something happen to Nina?" Meena whispered.

"No." He flipped through the service handout.

"Caroline?"

He clenched his jaw and concentrated real hard on the back sheet where the announcements were typed. But he didn't read them.

"Ooh, you two had a fight," she said. "Did you break up?"

"We were never together to begin with," he whispered harshly. "Just drop it."

One thing his cousin wasn't good at was dropping any juicy gossip.

"You two couldn't keep your eyes off each other—"

Thankfully, the pastor began speaking, and Meena focused ahead. Seth tried to listen, but his mind wandered. Why would Meena think he and Caroline were a couple? They hadn't been on any dates. He'd trained Spud. Showed her and Nina what to do. Had a meal at the ranch to celebrate. Big deal.

But it was a big deal. Introducing her to the squad had been a big deal for him. He'd enjoyed watching her interact with his siblings and cousins. The bonfire had drawn him closer—and the kiss after? Not a friendly peck on the cheek.

They might not be a couple, but his heart sure hadn't gotten the memo.

Why had he allowed himself to get so close to her? And why hadn't he prepared himself better for her inevitable blowup? She had trust issues when it came to him, and he'd probably never know why.

The service progressed, and Seth turned his attention to the sermon. Something about Thomas the disciple.

The pastor stood at the lectern. "We know him as doubting Thomas, but he was also courageous. He's credited as saying, 'Let us also go, that we may die with him,' when not long prior Jesus shared his intent to return to Judea, where he'd almost been stoned. After Jesus died, Thomas had a trust problem. He needed concrete evidence that his Lord, indeed, had arisen."

Seth could understand that.

"How did Jesus respond to His disciple? With anger? No. With patience and kindness. Jesus urged Thomas to touch the wounds in His hands and in His side. And with that, Thomas believed."

Okay, what was the pastor getting at?

"We live by faith," the pastor continued. "And we have a Savior who sympathizes with our weaknesses and shows us mercy."

The congregation rose to sing, and Seth stood but didn't bother joining in. Had he been patient with Caroline? Kind? Merciful?

Seth liked to think of himself as all those things. With Caroline, though, he'd had too much to lose, and he'd known it from the get-go. He'd given her the dog, trained him, spent all that time with her and Nina—he'd been patient and kind and merciful. And for what? To be told he wasn't reliable? To be yelled at for not calling her?

He wasn't perfect. Far from it. But he wasn't an irresponsible kid, either.

As the service wound down, the congregation prayed the Lord's Prayer, and he stumbled over the forgiveness part. His conscience whispered to ask for forgiveness. But why? He hadn't done anything wrong. If anyone needed forgiveness, it was Caroline.

When it was over, he waited for Meena to exit the pew, then followed her down the aisle to the large room where people stood chatting.

An older woman with short brown hair stopped him. "Say, aren't you the Hudson boy who's opening the dog-boarding center?"

"Yes." He wasn't in the mood to play nice—he wanted to leave. Try to forget he was a moron for falling for Caroline.

"I was so happy to hear it. I have two giant schnauzers, and I am tired of driving an hour to board them. When will the center be open?"

"Giant schnauzers, huh?" This was better. A potential customer. "Smart, loyal dogs."

"That they are," she said. "And they have a lot of energy."

"They'll love running around outside at the center. I have

enrichment activities indoors and outdoors for the dogs who board with us."

"When did you say it will be open?"

"Beginning of September."

"Good. I'm ready to book both dogs for the last week in September. I'm heading to the East Coast for a color tour with old friends. How do I sign my darlings up?"

His spirits boosted. "I'll have an online system in place in the next couple of days. It's almost ready to go. My cousin here—" Seth reached out and grabbed Cooper's sleeve "—helped me get it set up."

"Get what set up?" Cooper stood next to him.

"The software so Miss—what was your name?"

"Peggy Rutherford."

"Nice to meet you, Peggy." Seth offered her his hand. She shook it, clearly delighted.

"And I'm Cooper." His cousin held out his hand, which she shook, chuckling.

"That center of yours will be full all the time with you two handsome fellas around." Her eyes danced with mischief.

He glanced at Cooper, who gave a slight shrug.

"You should have an open house." Peggy pointed to him. "Let everyone see the center and meet you boys."

"That's a good idea. I'll keep it in mind." He thanked her again and pivoted to leave. He glanced at Coop. "I'm taking off. Think I'll head to the office and get the printer and everything set up. Then people like Peggy can actually start booking their dogs' stays."

"I've got nothing to do. I'll help." They walked outside into the sunshine. "Have you started advertising yet?"

"No. I have a marketing plan, but I haven't done much with it."

"Understandable. You've been busy."

He had been busy. Busy training Spud. Busy spending all

his free time with Caroline and Nina. Busy ignoring the fact he had a new business to launch.

"Yeah, well, it's time I buckled down and got started." As much as he wished he didn't have to create social media accounts for Hudson K-9 Center, he wouldn't mind the distraction.

At the moment, his heart wasn't really into boarding dogs. It was in a bungalow four blocks away where a beautiful single mom lived with her diabetic little girl.

"Let's go." He'd better get working on forgetting Caroline. He'd wasted enough time as it was. Back to reality. Starting now.

"We missed church, Mommy."

Caroline's head pounded. Her elbows rested on the kitchen table, and she struggled to lift the coffee mug to her lips. "I know, sweetheart. I overslept."

"Don't you feel good?" Nina stood next to her and put her tiny palm against Caroline's temple.

"My head hurts today."

"Do you have to take a shot?"

"No," she said, smiling, "I'll take an ibuprofen."

Spud ambled over, wagging his tail and smiling at her. Caroline petted behind his furry ears. "Nina, honey, can you give Spud his breakfast?"

"Come on, Spud! Time to eat!" She skipped away to the plastic bin where they stored his kibble. Caroline rested the side of her head against her palm and took another sip of coffee.

She'd been up until the wee hours of the morning. Her thoughts had tumbled over each other. Regrets chased around and around. She'd justified her actions. Then kicked herself for treating Seth the way she had. Then told herself she'd had every right to be angry at him and her father.

It had been useless. She had no closure.

She had no Seth.

And she wasn't sure what to do about it.

A knock on the front door startled her, and her coffee sloshed on the table.

"I'll get it, Mommy!" Nina yelled.

"No, I'll get it. You know you're not allowed to answer the front door." She pushed back from the table and slowly made her way to the entrance. *Please don't let it be Seth.* As she opened it, she couldn't help wishing it *was* Seth. Just showed how messed up she was.

"Dad. What are you doing here?"

"Grandpa!" Nina wiggled through and put her arms around his legs.

"Hey, there, Nina ballerina." He lifted her into his arms and gave Caroline a questioning look. "Can I come in?"

She nodded and stepped aside. In the living room, he gave Nina a kiss on the cheek before setting her on her feet.

"Why don't you make sure Spud's okay?" Caroline jerked her head to the kitchen, and Nina nodded, racing away. "Why didn't you call me yesterday, Dad?"

"I left a note." His eyebrows drew together. "I tell you, Darren gave me a scare."

"How is he?" She had basic manners. She could at least inquire about his friend.

"Stable. He passed out. The doctors ran tests—it's his heart."

"Was it a heart attack?" She turned and headed to the kitchen. Her father followed. She ripped off a few paper towels and wiped up the spilled coffee.

"No. Heart failure. They're putting him on meds. He should be all right."

Caroline took a seat at the table again, and her dad sat, too.

"I'm glad to hear that." And she was glad. "But, Dad, I needed you to call me. You should have told me Nina was with Seth."

"You told me I could count on Seth for a backup. He's spent

so much time with the dog and Nina, I don't know why you have a problem with it."

"I don't have a problem with him watching her. I have a problem with you not telling me. I was worried all day. That you wouldn't know what to do."

"I'm a grown man." His expression turned stern. "You left me detailed instructions. It wasn't that complicated."

"It is complicated!" She didn't mean to raise her voice. "Diabetes is complicated. It means giving her insulin, checking her glucose monitor, making sure she's not overheated or overtired. You act like it's no big deal."

"What do you want me to say?" He blinked a few times. "I'm not going to smother my granddaughter when everything's fine. Now, if that monitor would have beeped or Spud would have come up to me, I'd have taken action."

"That's not the point." She had to fight from balling her hands into fists.

"Then what is? Why are you so upset?"

Because I can't trust you! I can't trust anyone.

Her breath caught in her throat. That couldn't be true. She trusted her father. She trusted Seth.

But snippets of their argument last night rushed back. Seth's reckless words: *I forgot, Caroline. You can't trust me. Never could. I killed your dog, after all.*

"Caroline?" her father asked. "What are you so afraid of?"

Losing her. Losing my baby.

"Nina's my everything, Dad."

"I know." He reached over and patted her hand. "But I'm not the enemy. You've been self-reliant since your mother died, and I'm proud of you for keeping it together, getting a good job, raising Nina. But I wonder if all that holding it together has been good for you. You're brittle. And I don't want you to break."

"I'm not brittle. I'm not breaking," she snapped. Her hold

on the mug's handle tightened. "I'm responsible. I have a child with complicated health problems."

"Health problems that are under control." His gaze sliced her.

"Yes, because I make sure they're under control."

"And when she goes to daycare, you're constantly checking your phone to see her readings. And when she goes to school, you'll call the teacher so often, she'll want to quit. This worry isn't going to disappear."

"That's not true." She did stand then, and the throbbing in her head almost made her sit right back down. "Nina's got her CGM. She has Spud. I'm working on the babysitter situation. It will all be fine."

As she said it, though, she recognized the lie.

His eyebrows rose. "I hope you believe that. I really do, Caroline, because you're going to drive away people who care about you if you can't get the idea out of your head that you alone can prevent anything from happening to your daughter. Look at what happened to your mother. No one could have prevented it. That alone should convince you to stop holding on so tightly. Now I'm going to spend some time with Nina." He stood and left the room.

Her mother. The car accident. On a beautiful summer day like today. No reason. A truck swerved into her lane to avoid an animal and her mother swerved to miss the truck. Her car flipped over twice. She'd died instantly.

Her father was right. No one could have prevented it.

And then after the funeral, Lucy had been torn apart by coyotes. The puppies eaten. For no good reason. A young boy had wanted to see the pups and had been careless. Apparently, no one could have prevented that, either.

Pointless. Senseless.

Why had her mom died? Why had Lucy been torn apart?

Caroline had no answers.

But Nina…she *could* prevent her disease from killing her.

She didn't have to sit around waiting for the worst to happen. Didn't they all get that?

I'm only one woman. I'm trying so hard...

The pastor's sermon from a few weeks ago came to mind. He'd spoken about giving your burdens to God. That Jesus would take them and give you peace.

Yeah, well, she'd trusted God her entire life, and He'd still taken her mother from her with no warning. He'd taken Lucy and the pups.

How did she know He wasn't going to rip Nina from her, too?

Caroline let her head drop into her hands. *God, I don't know what to do. I'm scared. I'm terrified Nina will die, and I don't think anyone knows how serious her health is to me.*

That wasn't entirely true. Seth did. He'd given her a service dog. Sacrificed hours to train Spud. He'd been patient, understanding.

And she'd accused him—once again—of negligence. Both times she'd been wrong.

No wonder he'd told her their relationship was over. He'd already given her a do-over once. He wasn't going to give her another.

Nina's giggles and her dad's laughter drifted to her. Her dad was right. She needed to work on her trust issues. And she needed to apologize to Seth. But first, she needed to spend some time in prayer and ask Jesus for some of that peace He promised. She needed God now more than ever. She just hoped His mercy would extend to her.

Chapter Thirteen

"That should do it." Seth crawled out from under the desk in the boarding center's office a few hours after church.

"I'll boot it up." Cooper had finished hooking up the laptop to the internet, and the two of them had plugged in surge protectors, set up the printer and made sure the cords were tucked away where no one could trip over them. Additionally, Cooper had downloaded the software for the doggy cams that had been installed throughout the center for people to watch their dogs play.

"Is it working?" Seth straightened, brushing off his jeans and leaning over Cooper's shoulder to stare at the laptop's screen.

"Give it a minute." Coop's cell phone rang, and he checked it. "I've got to take this. I'll be back in a few."

"Go ahead." Seth waved him off. He hadn't expected it to take so long to get all the equipment set up. He still needed to create the social media accounts and work on advertisements. While he had some experience with social media working for his previous employer, he was no expert.

Being here wasn't quite the distraction he needed. Every time he completed a task, Caroline's frantic face would appear in his mind. Her panic when she'd rushed to check Nina on the couch. Her temper as he tried to explain.

And instead of feeling defensive, he felt sorry for her.

What was it like to live in a constant state of fear? To never quite trust anyone—even those closest to you?

The love he felt for her hurt his heart. She refused to recognize the problem, and he would have to make peace with that at some point.

They weren't meant for each other. Period.

"Hi."

The soft female voice had him spinning on his heels. Caroline stood in the doorway. Her long hair hung down her back, and her big brown eyes were full of remorse.

"I didn't expect to see you." He stood rigid near the desk.

"No, I suppose you wouldn't. Can I come in?"

He barely recognized the subdued woman who wafted in. She stopped and rested her hand on the back of the chair he'd put together yesterday. He'd never seen her so crestfallen.

"I came to apologize."

He didn't try to hide his surprise as his eyebrows arched. He wasn't going to make this easy on her, because it really didn't matter. She could apologize. Wouldn't change anything.

She attempted a smile, but it only made her look on the verge of tears. *Don't feel sorry for her. Don't do it.*

"I'm sorry for all the hurtful things I said yesterday. I should have thanked you for taking care of Nina while I was gone. You got my dad out of a bind—and me, too. He appreciated it. And I appreciate it." Each word came out tentative, as if she wasn't sure how to string the words together. "I don't know why I have so many trust issues, Seth."

Okay, now she was starting to get to him. His stance softened a notch. "Do you have any theories?"

"Yeah. A few." She nodded, her eyes glimmering with unshed tears. "Before Mom died, I never gave much thought about losing the people closest to me."

He could relate to that.

"But she was taken so suddenly. So unexpectedly. And then

Lucy was so savagely killed. And the puppies. It didn't make sense."

He almost interrupted. Wanted to tell her he'd had nothing to do with it. That it wasn't his fault.

She shivered. "I blamed you—I made no secret of it. And I regretted it immediately."

"Why didn't you say anything at the time? You could have called. Apologized. You cut me out of your life. And we'd been close, Caroline. We'd been falling for each other even back then."

"I know." Her eyes closed briefly, and then she stared at him. "I thought I was losing everyone. I can't explain it, but it felt like at any moment, everyone I loved would be taken from me. I should have called you. Should have apologized. But maybe it was easier for me not to. Then I'd never have to worry about a phone call from the police that you were dead, too."

"That's why you never called? You figured I'd die, so why bother?"

"You asked for theories. I don't know." She raised her palms as she shook her head. "I just don't know."

"I appreciate your apology. And I'm glad you figured out… whatever it is you figured out. But it doesn't change anything."

She nodded, averting her gaze. "I know. I didn't expect it would. I still owed you an apology. And more. I know this isn't what you want to hear. I also know it's over between us. But I have to tell you I love you. I'm sorry, Seth. I'm not good at this. But I loved you back then, and I love you now. And I'm so sorry I hurt you."

How he'd longed to hear those words from her. He wished he could forgive her and move on. Pretend like nothing had happened. But it had happened. And he couldn't give her his heart unless he was certain she wouldn't stomp all over it.

"It's good of you to tell me all that, Caroline." He swallowed, willing himself to be strong. "But your behavior makes me question your love. And I can't trust that you won't hurt me again. So this isn't going to be one of those 'all is forgiven and let's ride off into the sunset' moments. It's obvious you don't think too highly of me, and I won't be waiting around for you to accuse me of the worst again, no matter how much I love you. And I do love you. I'll watch Spud for you every day until you get a babysitter, but that's it. We're done."

She tried to nod, but the tears dripping down her cheeks made her look like the saddest person he'd ever seen. "I understand. I do. I deserve that. I'll get out of here." Caroline held her head high as she turned and left. Cooper passed her as he came back into the room.

"Is she okay?" Coop frowned.

Seth couldn't tell him she was. She wasn't okay. He wasn't, either. He hadn't expected her to apologize, but words weren't enough. He needed action. And until he saw proof she'd changed, he didn't see a future for them.

"I overheard the last part of the conversation." Cooper took a seat and rolled it to the desk where the laptop was set up. The keyboard clicked as he typed. "She seemed pretty sincere."

Great. He'd heard everything. "I don't want to talk about it."

"Hey, I get it. You don't trust her. And why would you?" He tossed him a knowing backward glance. "But you admitted you love her. And she loves you. And she apologized."

"Drop it." The dog trainer in him couldn't help but use the command. "She thinks she loves me, and yes, she apologized, but she hasn't convinced me."

"What do you mean?" The clicking stopped, and the laptop screen glowed in green and orange colors as the software icon appeared.

He hadn't told anyone about their fight last night. Wasn't anyone's business. Plus, it embarrassed him. But this was Coop. His best friend.

"When she picked up Nina last night, she said a lot of hurtful things."

"Like what? Why would she be mad?" The mouse clicked as Cooper skipped through screens until pulling up the settings.

"Ken told me he had let Caroline know he was leaving Nina with me. And he said not to disturb her during training. So I didn't."

"But he didn't tell her?"

"No. He left a note. And it said something like he was at the hospital and to call me."

"And she assumed he'd had to take Nina to the hospital."

"I guess. I don't know. Caroline came in hot and said a lot of things. Acted like I was a monster for letting Nina help with the insulin shots. Ranted that I should have texted her to let her know what was going on. And the way she twisted my words?" He shifted his jaw and stared up at the ceiling. "I'm done with her."

"Wasn't like this was the first time she let her temper get out of control. Sounds like you're better off without her."

"I don't know..." Why had he admitted that? "This time—it felt different, I guess."

"She *did* apologize." Cooper spun on the chair to face him.

"Yeah."

"And she told you she loves you. I heard it myself."

"I suppose." He sighed.

"We all like Caroline, Seth. And Nina, too. Maybe you should pray about it before cutting her out of your life."

And if he prayed about it and she hurt him again?

Why would he risk it? He was tired of being in this situation. Love wasn't for him.

Sobs erupted from Caroline as she drove to her father's house. She'd ruined her relationship with Seth. And too late, she'd finally realized how much he meant to her.

She'd never met anyone like him. Self-sacrificing, kind,

strong, intelligent, patient—the man oozed patience. And instead of appreciating him, she'd treated him like a dumb kid. She didn't blame him for ending things. Maybe he was right to pull the plug.

She'd hurt him twice. If they continued to see each other, she'd only hurt him again.

Instead of driving straight to her dad's, the gazebo called her name. She pulled into a parking spot, grabbed a tissue and dabbed under her eyes, then blew her nose. She needed to think. To get some fresh air. To figure out why she kept assuming the worst and find a way to start assuming the best.

Caroline strolled through the grass to the gazebo and found a seat on a bench inside. The blue sky should have lifted her mood, but guilt weighed it down.

I don't know who I am anymore, God. I had my whole life planned before Mom died. Then I hurt Seth so spectacularly and escaped Fairwood. Ever since, I've been pushing myself forward, and I don't even know where the path I'm on leads. I'm so confused.

A breeze kissed her face, and the sound of children laughing on the playground eased her heart. She didn't have to stay stuck. Just because she'd botched the best thing that had happened to her since adopting Nina didn't mean life was over.

She'd make a list. Figure it out.

Swiping her phone, she brought up the app she used for lists. Almost every item had been checked with a note next to it.

Find a service dog for Nina. (Seth Hudson)
Look into taking out a loan to pay for dog. (No loan needed)
Fill out paperwork for school. (July 15)
Look for ways to add value to job. (Training)
Spend more time with Dad. (Friday night suppers)
Manicure—every week! Nonnegotiable.
Figure out a thank-you gift for Seth.

She created a new note and typed out a list.

Surrender Nina's health to God.
Treat my loved ones with respect.
Figure out how to thank Seth.
Tell Nina she's adopted.

Caroline set her phone aside. How could she show Seth she appreciated him? She'd thanked him repeatedly for getting Spud and training him. As of right now, Seth clearly didn't want to see her or interact with her.

Maybe he needed time.

Maybe she did, too. She couldn't pretend she'd be able to change in one second. The anxiety and worry that assaulted her during times of extreme stress made her lash out. And she didn't want to lash out anymore.

She added another item to her list. Look up techniques to cope with stress.

No time like the present. She typed in a search, skimming the results until she came to one that intrigued her. It offered Bible-based tips. She selected it and began reading.

Stress produces anger? She was living proof of that. The tips—slow down, show mercy, own your mistakes, give it to God, know your triggers—all resonated with her, and the practical advice wasn't difficult to understand. She shared the link to her note-taking app to review later.

Why hadn't she done anything about her stress years ago?

She rose, slipping the phone into her purse. She was finally willing to face ugly truths. She wanted—needed—control over every aspect of her life because she believed everyone would let her down. But striving for perfection had produced false beliefs. That her way was right and every other way was wrong.

Instead of leaving the gazebo, she closed her eyes and prayed. *Lord, what's the point of being right if everyone I love hates me?*

Maybe it was time to loosen her grip on how she was raising Nina. And show some grace to the people who loved her. And maybe even show some grace to herself.

Caroline made her way back to the minivan. And her thoughts returned to the article about coping with stress as she drove to her father's house. If she could reduce her stress, she'd be less likely to have angry outbursts. And if she did the things the article mentioned about showing mercy and giving it to God, maybe she'd have a chance at truly managing her fear.

Her thoughts built on each other until she parked in her dad's driveway. She found him out back. Nina was sleeping on a lounger in the shade with Spud dozing on the ground next to her. Caroline dropped into one of the patio chairs.

"You look rough, kiddo." He pushed himself out of his chair and came over to her, dropping a kiss on the top of her head like he used to when she was young. The gesture made the backs of her eyes prickle. "I feel bad about yesterday, and I thought about what you said. I should have called you. Nina *is* important, and I understand why you worry. I was so caught up with Darren, I didn't think about you. Want a lemonade?" He pointed to the patio door.

"Sure, Dad. And you don't need to apologize. You were in a tough situation, and you handled it well. You got Nina to someone who would care for her properly, and you still managed to help your friend."

"That's good of you to say, but I was wrong. I can admit it. Give me one sec." He slid open the door and disappeared inside.

Her dad had apologized? Usually he brushed off her concerns as *worrying too much* or *overthinking things again*. For him to acknowledge her feelings felt like a major step forward.

Soon, he set a glass of lemonade on the table next to her. The ice cubes crackled as she thanked him.

"I've realized I might be a control freak." She quirked the

corner of her mouth as she gave him a sideways glance. "I need to work on it."

"Nah." He settled back into his chair. "You're on top of things."

"That's a nice way to put it."

"Don't be so hard on yourself. You're dealing with a lot. The move, Nina's diabetes, the dog, Seth. What's going on between you two, anyhow?"

"Nothing." She jiggled the glass and took a sip. "I ruined that, too. Again."

"Want to tell me what happened?"

"Not really."

He nodded, gazing out at the backyard. "I'm here if you change your mind."

Not knowing what to say, she took note of the tart and sweet sensations on her tongue from the lemonade.

"You know Seth is used to helping dogs learn special skills. Takes time to train them. He doesn't expect perfection. Just progress."

"Are you comparing me to a dog being trained?" She almost choked on the drink. Where was her dad going with this?

"No. I'm saying he understands when a dog—or a human—makes a mistake."

"That may be true, but I made one mistake too many." She sank into the chair until her head rested against the back. "Even service dogs get cut from the program if they don't perform to expectations."

Great. Now *she* was comparing herself to a dog. How low could she go today? Not low enough, apparently.

Her dad chuckled. "Yeah, I suppose you're right, but Seth—he's good for you. And you're good for him."

She straightened again, her shoulders tensing. "How would you know if we're good for each other? You haven't seen us together except for Spud's testing."

The dog raised his chin from his paws at his name, then settled once more.

"I saw it when you were a teenager, and I see it now. Give him some time. He'll come around."

"What if he doesn't?"

He leveled an intense stare her way. "You'll have to show him that you two are good for each other."

"What if we aren't?" She couldn't help thinking Seth deserved someone better. Someone who wouldn't throw nasty accusations at him whenever life got tough.

"Why? What did he do?" He shot to attention. "I thought he respected you, but—"

"Dad, I wasn't talking about Seth. I was talking about me. What if I'm not good for him?"

"Why would you say that? You've spent the summer together."

"He kind of had to—the dog, you know."

"Bah. If he didn't like being with you, he wouldn't have been spending time with you each night."

"Again, training."

"The dog didn't need *that* much training." He grunted. "Why do you find it so hard to believe he cares for you?"

She opened her mouth, but no words formed, so she shut it.

"You're worthy of love, you know. You're worthy of *his* love. So you messed up? Your mother and I had some nasty fights. We said things we wished we could have taken back."

"How did you two get past it?"

"Sometimes it took a while. Most of the time, your mother was the bigger person than me. She didn't hold a grudge—not for long, anyhow. When I was younger, I didn't appreciate her the way I should have. I miss her. She accepted me, loved me, was my best friend. I haven't had that since she died."

Caroline felt that way about Seth. Could her dad be right?

That her mistake wasn't catastrophic? That Seth could forgive her enough to let her in again? He'd said he loved her…

"You've given me a lot to think about, Dad."

"Don't go overthinking, now."

She didn't respond. They both knew she specialized in overthinking. But, unlike in the past, she didn't want to think this situation to death.

She was going to take action. Her dad was right. She'd give Seth time, but she wouldn't sit idle, either. It was time to show him that she could change, that she respected him, needed him and loved him.

And if he still wanted nothing to do with her?

She wanted a full life—with Seth in it. And she wasn't backing down until she got it.

Chapter Fourteen

His final day with Spud. Friday night, almost two weeks later, Seth drove down Hickory Street on his way to Caroline's. Spud and Liverwurst sat in the back seat. He checked the time—a few minutes after six, when he typically dropped off Spud. Tonight was the last time he'd be dropping off the dog. And he wished it wasn't.

Caroline had hired Fran Bolenski to babysit Nina, and Fran would be starting on Monday. He, Caroline, Nina and Spud had spent the past two evenings at Fran's duplex two blocks away to get her and Spud used to each other and for Fran to pick up on Spud's cues. Caroline had also gone over Nina's insulin dosing, the CGM and her schedule. The woman seemed ideal to watch Nina.

Seth hadn't lingered either time. He'd left as soon as he felt Fran understood the dog's alerts. But he'd wanted to stay.

Every morning when he picked up Spud, Caroline greeted him at the door and handed him a brown lunch bag as he collected the dog. Nina, of course, ran to him and gave him a hug. Man, he loved those hugs. After leaving, he'd head to the center, check the progress and open the paper bag as he played fetch with the dogs out back.

The bag's contents were the same each day—an apple, a homemade muffin, three Hershey's kisses and a handwritten note.

The notes had surprised him. The first day, he almost didn't read the note, but curiosity had gotten the best of him, and he'd unfolded it and gotten caught up in her words. In the first letter, she'd apologized again and explained how she was working on her control issues. She told him how Nina couldn't stop talking about her fun day with him, and she opened up about what a blessing his friendship was to her.

The second day, the note had gotten more personal, with her admiring his work ethic and patience. Then she'd shared how difficult she found it to give her worries to the Lord. Her self-deprecating humor had made him smile. The Caroline in the notes was the woman he'd fallen in love with, and he found himself missing the time they'd spent together.

By day three, he'd taken to tearing the bag open in the truck at the center before checking the progress or playing with the dogs. He looked forward to the notes that much. But every night when he dropped off Spud, he didn't mention them. Hadn't given her a hint how much they meant to him. And he wasn't sure why.

Seth turned at the four-way stop. Only a few blocks to go.

As each day passed, with another brown paper bag and another note, Seth had realized he was wrong to stay silent. He'd been praying nonstop, and his thoughts kept returning to the disciple Thomas. How the pastor had said Thomas doubted, yes, but he also had courage. And how Jesus had been patient with His beloved disciple.

The whole thing kept poking Seth's conscience. Wasn't he the same as Thomas? Telling Caroline he'd only believe her if he had proof she'd changed? He hadn't really forgiven her for hurting him. All he'd done was try to protect himself.

And after two weeks of her snacks and notes, Seth could no longer deny that Caroline made his life better, not worse.

He needed her. He missed her. And he wanted her in his life permanently.

He was willing to take a chance on Caroline Bright, with all her lists and worries. If she needed extra communication while he had Nina, he'd text her every hour. If she worried about having all of Nina's supplies on hand when they went to the park, he'd pack an extra bag himself.

Caroline needed more understanding and more help from him.

His mind went back to the day of her mom's funeral. When he thought about standing there as she'd screamed and yelled at him, he couldn't help wishing he'd reacted differently. Maybe what she'd really needed was his arms around her, the chance to cry and let it all out.

But he'd left.

And maybe what she needed now was the same. Instead of dismissing her worries and distancing himself from her, he'd take the time to listen to them and help her however he could.

As her driveway came into view, his palms grew sweaty. He'd put on clean jeans, his best cowboy boots, a dark short-sleeved shirt and, of course, his favorite cowboy hat. He'd also gone behind Caroline's back and asked Ken if he'd babysit Nina for a couple of hours. Ken had jumped at the chance and had called him ten minutes ago to let him know the coast was clear.

After parking, Seth got out and let the dogs out of the back seat, then took a deep breath, squared his shoulders and headed up her front porch. He figured since she'd been writing him all those notes, she still loved him. But he wasn't sure. Maybe he'd pushed her away. Maybe friendship was all she could handle.

He'd take what he could get at this point.

Before he knocked, the front door opened, and the pinched expression on her face had him concerned.

"What's wrong?" he asked.

The dogs wagged their tails as they sauntered inside, and he followed.

She shook her head, closing the door. "Nothing. Dad picked up Nina a few minutes ago, and I wasn't thinking. I guess I forgot that this is it. The last time you'll drop off Spud. And Nina's not even here to thank you and say goodbye. I shouldn't have let Dad take her. I don't know what I was thinking."

"Hey, it's okay. I asked Ken to take her." Seth wanted to pull her into his arms and smooth his hand down her hair, but he kept his hands to himself. "I wanted to talk to you alone."

"Oh?" She began picking at one of her nails. Must have realized it, too, because she balled her hands into fists and shoved them down by her sides. "Want to sit down?"

"Yeah." He crossed over to the couch. All the things he'd planned on saying were jumbling up in his mind.

"For the record, I'm not worried about Dad watching Nina. I want you to know that," she said quickly. "I feel bad because she adores you, and you won't be around anymore, and she'll miss you. I've been trying to prepare her, but—"

"Caroline." He ached for what she was putting herself through. "It's going to be okay. I needed to talk to you. That's all."

"About what?"

He patted the couch next to him, and she sat beside him with her hands in her lap, her thumb chipping away at the polish on her nail. He shifted to speak to her directly.

"The bags with the notes you've been sending every day—they mean a lot to me."

Her throat worked as she swallowed. "I'm glad."

"I look forward to your letters. I feel like I'm getting to know a whole different part of you."

"It's weird, huh?" The chipping continued. "I'm not used to opening up like that."

"It's not weird." He reached up and tucked a few stray tendrils of hair behind her ear. "It's special. I can't wait to read them, and when I do, I wish they were longer."

"You do?" Her hands stilled.

"Yeah."

"But you didn't say anything."

"I know. I'm sorry. I wasn't ready. I've been praying a lot about us, and I owe you an apology."

Caroline got to her feet, turning away from him. "No, you don't."

"Yes, I do." He stood, too, and put his arm around her, turning her to face him. "I wanted you on my terms, and I was overlooking what you needed."

"That's not true. You've been patient and generous and respectful."

"Caroline, you lashed out because you were scared. Terrified, I'm sure. And I should have recognized it. I wish I'd taken you in my arms and held you."

"You should have run away as far as possible. I was awful. I don't know why you ever agreed to help me with Spud. I didn't deserve it."

He put his hands on her shoulders and bent to look into her eyes. "That's where you're wrong. You do deserve it. You've always deserved it. I loved you then, and I wish I'd been more mature. I wish I'd seen your grief and not taken what you said to heart. You'd have seen things more rationally. I know you would have."

Tears began streaming from her eyes as she shook her head. "Stop making excuses for me."

"I'm not. I'm seeing the past through a different lens. And I wish I'd had this insight a few weeks ago when I watched Nina for your dad."

"You weren't in the wrong. I was." She jabbed her thumb into her chest.

"Caroline, I know you. I know your heart is filled with love for Nina, and I know how much you worry about her health. We've spent enough time together all summer for me to know I should have texted you and kept you in the loop while you were gone. I let you down. I'm sorry."

"Stop it!" She wrenched out of his arms. "I'm the bad guy, Seth. Me. Not you."

He wasn't letting her emotionally push him away again. Love for her made him move in closer. "You're not bad, Caroline. You're good. So good. I want to be here for you. The way you need me to be. I don't want you to feel like you have to apologize for caring about Nina or Spud or your dad or anyone. I'll support you better. I promise."

"What are you saying, Seth?" Anguish mixed with hope in her pretty brown eyes.

"I'm saying I love you."

"But I'm a control freak."

"Says who? I see a mom wanting to keep her daughter safe."

"The lists—"

"I like your lists." He moved even closer, but she shook her head. "I've always loved them."

"I thought I could do this. But I can't."

His heart fell to the floor with a thud. He'd thought they were on the same page. Was he too late?

Caroline tried to untangle her thoughts as she rubbed her biceps. Seth stood a foot away, and she didn't dare look into his eyes, because she knew she'd only see the pain and disappointment she'd caused twice in the past.

"I can't put you through this again," she whispered.

"Put me through what?"

"Me. My temper. I try to keep a lid on it, but I know I'll fly off the handle and accuse you of something awful. I will. We both know it."

"Yeah?" He shrugged. "I don't expect it will happen too often."

"How do you know? I could flip out tomorrow." She retreated a few inches. "Or Monday. Or two years from now. Or every day for the next decade. I'm worried about leaving Nina with Fran—and it makes no sense. Fran is more than qualified, adores kids and will give Nina the one-on-one supervision she needs."

"Sounds normal to me."

How could he smile and look at her with so much compassion and love? Why couldn't he take her word for it—she'd only hurt him?

"I know you're trying to push me away, Caroline. But it's no use. I love you, and I'm not going to give up on us. I'm not walking away. If you don't love me, that's different. But you told me you love me, and all the notes you've sent this past week and all the time we spent together this summer says you do. You and I can work out anything that comes our way."

"You mean it, don't you?" she asked. The yawning hole inside her began to close. This was a man she could lean on. A man who saw through her fears and wanted to stay. "I love you, too, Seth. I fell in love with you all over again this summer, and I didn't want to. I didn't want to get close."

"I didn't, either." He took her hand in his, gently rubbing it with his thumb. "I was afraid of getting hurt."

"And you did get hurt. I hurt you. I'm so sorry. There aren't enough apologies in the world—"

"I forgive you. It's over. As far as I'm concerned, we never have to discuss it again."

"Thank you." Tears formed as she nodded. "I have to ask—what about Nina?"

"What about Nina?" He wrapped his hands around her waist, and she had to tip her head back to look up at him.

"She adores you. I couldn't bear to get her hopes up only for something to happen and we break up."

Seth searched her eyes. "Nothing's going to happen. I don't give away my heart lightly. It's yours. For good."

He was saying all the right things, but there was still a snag, one thing keeping her from wrapping her arms around him and hugging him for dear life.

"I'm afraid to get the call, Seth," she whispered. "I'm so scared of getting the call like I did with my mom. I love you, and I don't think I can handle losing you."

His arms pulled her closer, and she rested her cheek against his chest. His heartbeat thumped through his shirt. "I worry about losing you, too, Caroline. And my family. Nina. We'll have to trust God with it."

"But that's the problem. I trusted Him, and He still took my mom."

He leaned back slightly to look in her eyes. "I don't know why her life was cut short, Caroline, but I do know she's with her Savior."

Caroline nestled into his embrace, wishing she could turn off the tears that kept coming. "I wish she was here. I miss her. I need her."

"I know." He stroked her hair. "I wish she was here, too. I guess that's part of love—missing them when they're gone."

His patience, his kindness, his comfort—all gave her the strength she needed. She pulled out of his embrace.

"Seth, I love you. And I want to get closer to you. I want to spend our evenings together, like we did this summer. You're amazing. I know the dog-boarding center will be successful, and you'll probably train a service dog here or there because you're good at it and you love it. I want to be as supportive to you as you are to me. Tell me what you need, and I'll do my best to help you."

"What do I need? Hmm." He glanced up, then stared at her with so much love, it took her breath away. "Well, the first thing I need is a kiss. Then I'm taking you out to dinner, because I need tacos and to hear everything that's going on with you."

"Is that all?" Her hands crept up his chest and slid around his neck.

"All? No. Then we'll pick up Nina and Spud and head over to the ranch to tell my family we're dating. I love you, beautiful." He lowered his mouth to hers, and she sank into his kiss, thrilled to be his, wanting him to know how deeply she cared for him.

And when he finally pulled away, she couldn't resist cupping her hand to his cheek. "I could get used to that."

"Noted." He grinned.

"What will we tell Nina?" She bit her lower lip.

"That we're in love, and that she's going to be seeing a lot more of me."

"I like the sound of that." She nodded. "And, just so you know, I think it's time I told her she's adopted."

"If you want, I'll be right by your side."

"You'd do that for me? Yes, I want you there. Tonight."

"So basically, I'm indispensable?"

"Yep. I don't know what I'd do without you."

"It's a good thing you won't have to find out."

Chapter Fifteen

Two hours later, Seth followed Caroline out to her dad's patio. Nina was sitting on Ken's lap as he read her a story. Spud had trotted over to sit next to them.

"Mommy!" Nina climbed down and ran into Caroline's arms. Seth's heart swelled at the sweet moment. He still couldn't quite believe Caroline loved him.

"Mr. Hudson!" Nina let go of her mom to wrap her arms around his legs. He hoisted her up on his hip. "Why are you here?"

He glanced at Caroline, hoping she'd take the lead on this one. Her big smile lit her eyes.

"Mr. Hudson and I are in love."

Nina's mouth formed an O as her eyes grew big. "Really? Does this mean you're going to be my daddy?"

Warmth crept up his neck, and once more he looked at Caroline. Her eyebrows rose as her eyes twinkled. He bopped Nina's nose and set her on her feet. "Someday I hope to be your daddy, but your mommy and I have to date a while first."

"You really *might* be my daddy?" She brought her clasped hands under her chin.

"It's more than likely. But not right away." Caroline gestured to the patio furniture. "I have something else to tell you, Nina. Why don't we sit down?"

"I'm glad to hear you two finally figured out you're perfect for each other." Ken's eyes were misty as he came over and held out his hand. Seth shook it. "You're a good one."

"Thanks, Ken." Seth found a seat at the table and took off his cowboy hat.

Caroline caressed Nina's arms as she stood in front of her.

"You're getting to be a big girl," Caroline said. "I think it's time you know a little more about your family."

"Like what?"

Caroline's sideway glance practically begged him to help her out.

Seth leaned forward. "Nina, you've asked a lot of questions lately about your father." The girl seemed pensive. "And your mom has some answers for you."

"Yes," Caroline coughed. "About your father—"

"Am I going to meet him?" Nina asked.

"No, I'm sorry, you won't be able to meet him." Her expression oozed remorse. "And it's only because I don't know who he is. You see, I adopted you when you were born."

"Adopted?" Nina's face scrunched like a raisin. "What's that?"

"It means I'm not your biological mother. I didn't give birth to you."

"Your tummy didn't get big like Yasmine's mommy's?" Nina seemed to be taking it in stride. Seth assumed Yasmine was a kid from daycare.

"No, another woman carried you in her tummy, but she couldn't keep you."

"Why not?" Her expression dimmed.

"She was young, and she wasn't ready for a baby, so I told her I'd love to raise you."

"She didn't want me?" Nina blinked a few times.

"Well…" Caroline met Seth's gaze over Nina's head and mouthed *help.*

"Nina, the woman who gave birth to you couldn't take care of you," Seth said. "She wanted you to have a good life and knew Caroline would love you. And so she adopted you."

Caroline looked relieved. "And I loved you before you were born. I couldn't imagine my life without you in it. I know you're going to have questions, and I'll try to answer them as best as I can."

"Are you ever not going to be my mommy? The other lady can't take me away, can she?"

"No, darling." Caroline pulled her into a hug, stroking her hair as she kissed the side of her head. "No one can ever take you away from me. I'll always be your mommy."

"I love you, Mommy." She hugged her tightly.

"I love you, too, Nina."

Nina stepped back with a look of wonder. "I have to tell Spud!"

"Okay." Caroline appeared shell-shocked as Nina went to the dog and sat cross-legged in front of him. While Nina explained the situation to Spud, Seth reached over and took Caroline's hand in his.

"You did a good job." He squeezed her hand. "Nervous?"

"Relieved." Her big smile burrowed in his heart. "You and Dad were right."

"I was right about something?" Ken laughed. "First time for everything, I guess."

"Don't say that, Dad," Caroline said. "I learned everything I needed to know from you and Mom."

"She'd be proud of you." Ken nodded before addressing Seth. "And she'd be happy you two are together."

"That means a lot to me." Seth had a feeling of everything falling into place. Like he was meant to be right here, right now, with Ken, Caroline, Nina and Spud. He could picture many more nights like this ahead.

"Oh, and Caroline?" Ken hitched his chin to her. "Check your phone."

She rummaged through her purse until she found the phone. Her eyes opened wide in astonishment. "You texted me?"

"Sure did." He leaned back with his hands behind his head.

"But how?"

"I got me a new phone." He slid it out of his pocket and pushed it across the table. "A smartphone. Dierdre from work showed me how to use it. I thought it would be more complicated than it is."

She rose, crossing over to her father, and gave him a long hug. "Thanks, Dad. I can't believe you finally got one."

"I should have gotten one sooner. Didn't realize—well, maybe I did—I guess I didn't see how you not being able to get ahold of me was affecting you."

"I really appreciate this." Her voice cracked with emotion. "I can't tell you how much it means to me."

"*You* mean the world to me. And Nina does, too. It was the least I could do. Now, how about a soda?"

"Actually, Dad, I think we're going to take Nina to the ranch."

"Good plan."

As Caroline helped Nina gather her things, Seth and Ken stood.

"You're an answer to a prayer, Seth."

"What do you mean?"

"I've prayed for a long time that Caroline would find a Christian man to love her. I rest easier knowing you're in the picture."

His words touched him. "Thank you. She's an answer to my prayer. I need your daughter. I love her, and I'll do my best to make her and Nina happy."

"I know you will. And I'm right here if you need anything."

Seth gave him a quick hug, put his cowboy hat back on and went inside to find Caroline. After saying goodbye to her dad and buckling Nina into her booster seat, Seth drove them to the ranch.

"Are we going to have a fire again, Mr. Hudson?" Nina asked

from the back seat. He glanced in the rearview and a wave of love hit him at the sight of her holding her stuffed bunny and Spud sitting next to her.

"We might."

"Yay! I like bonfires. I'm going to tell Jonah I'm adopted!"

"Good plan." He glanced at Caroline, and she smiled. Keeping one hand on the steering wheel, he reached over and squeezed her hand. "You did the right thing."

"Thanks. You were right about it." She stared ahead. "Do you think your family will be pleased? Or..."

"They'll be pleased." He stated it with confidence, but a small part of him worried how they'd react when he told them. Cooper, of course, was on board with them dating. Would the rest of the squad be, too? He'd tried to call Kylie earlier, but she hadn't picked up. He'd left her a quick voicemail with the details. Figured she'd have called back by now, but he hadn't exactly been checking his phone. If Kylie had a problem with Caroline, he'd just have to set her straight.

"What's the latest at work?" Seth asked.

"I've been asked to help research cases and prepare documents for the attorneys. I'm excited. Oh, and I got a raise."

"Nice."

They discussed her new job duties the rest of the way to the ranch. After parking, Seth let Spud out of the back seat while Caroline helped Nina get unbuckled. He slung his arm around Caroline's shoulders as they strolled up the lodge's front porch steps. Nina and Spud got there first.

Caroline paused at the front door. "I'm nervous."

"That makes two of us."

"Aren't we going in?" Nina asked.

"Yes." Seth opened the front door, and Nina and Spud surged inside. He took Caroline's face in his hands and lightly kissed her lips. "I love you. Are you ready for this?"

She nodded. "I'm ready for anything if you're with me."

He held her hand as they went down the hall to the living room. Nina had raced to Lillian, holding Jonah. The rest of the squad stopped talking as he and Caroline approached holding hands. Then Kylie entered the room. The silence felt unnatural. Explosive.

"What did I miss?" Kylie asked.

Seth's tongue grew thick, but then Caroline pressed his hand, and his nerves faded away.

"Caroline and I are officially dating." He beamed at her.

"And I'm adopted!" Nina yelled, all excited.

"Wow." Lillian set the baby on the floor, and he crawled to Nina. "You're adopted?"

"Yeah." She sounded proud. "I'm going to tell Jonah all about it."

Seth missed the rest of her words because the squad had surrounded them. Cooper congratulated him. Meena squealed as she hugged Caroline. Brody and Hayden both gave Caroline a quick hug, too.

"You're happy." Kylie waited for things to die down before coming over to Seth. "It's really good to see you happy."

"Thanks, Ky." He pulled her in for a big hug. "I appreciate that."

"I don't know if you remember me." She turned to Caroline and held her arms out. "I'm Kylie, and I think we're going to be good friends."

Caroline hugged her for a long moment, then stepped back and glanced his way, blinking as if she hadn't expected such a warm reception.

"I hope so," Caroline said. "I'm looking forward to getting to know you better."

"Why don't you introduce me to your little girl? Nina, right?"

"I'd love to." They walked away, and Hayden and Brody came over.

"She's great, man. I'm glad you worked it out." Brody stood tall.

"I am, too. Best thing that's ever happened to me."

"You're sure about this." Hayden wore his serious expression, as usual.

"I'm sure."

Hayden nodded. "That's all I needed to hear."

"So what's this about Nina being adopted?" Cooper asked.

"We'll talk about it later. Nina requested a bonfire."

"A bonfire?" Brody rubbed his hands together. "Now we're talking. I'll get the chairs ready."

"I'll get the logs." Hayden was already on his way down the hall.

"I'm fanning the flames this time." Cooper loped away.

"Not a chance!" Brody and Hayden yelled in unison.

"I'll get the bug spray." Meena hustled after them. "Are you coming, Lil?"

Lillian picked up Jonah, who began to cry. "We'll be there. Let me change his diaper first."

"Let's go out and make sure the boys know what they're doing." Kylie held her hand out to Nina, who gazed up at her in awe as she giggled. "And bring Spud, too."

"Come on, Spud. Oh, wait." Nina looked back at Caroline. "Is it okay if I go outside?"

"Of course," Caroline said. "Thank Ms. Kylie, first."

"Thanks, Ms. Kylie."

"You're welcome." Kylie turned to Caroline. "I'm a nursing assistant. She's in safe hands with me."

"I'm not worried." Caroline sidled up next to Seth. "Seth has told me all about you. Thanks for being so kind to her."

"She's adorable." Kylie flushed as she smiled. "Well, I'll see you outside."

"Looks like it's just us." Seth put his arm around Caroline's waist and spun her to face him.

"That went well."

"It did." He stared into her eyes, pleased everyone had been so welcoming. "I love you, Caroline."

"I love you, too." She beamed.

"And since we're all alone…" He gave her a long, lingering kiss. "I've been wanting to do that for some time."

"It's only been an hour." She laughed, swatting at his chest.

"An hour? Feels like it's been months." He kissed her again. "There. That's better."

"Keep it up and we won't make it out to the bonfire."

"The squad has everything under control."

"Do they now?" She had her hands on his shoulders and so much love in her eyes, it took his breath away.

"I'm glad we're together." He rested his forehead against hers.

"Me, too."

The mudroom door slammed. "Are you two coming out here or not?" Meena shouted.

Seth laughed and offered Caroline his hand. "Shall we?"

She placed her hand in his. And he knew they'd work through any problems just like this—facing them together.

Epilogue

Was he ready to say goodbye to his bachelor life?

Yep. He sure was. On a cold day in October, Seth closed the square jewelry box and slipped it in his pants pocket. The past couple of months had been memorable. He'd moved into the house and opened Hudson K-9 Center at the end of August. The center was already booked through Christmas. He'd had so many requests for doggy daycare, he'd immediately added the service and hired two employees. Managing the center and hanging out with dogs all day fulfilled him more than he'd thought possible.

And spending his free time with Caroline and Nina fulfilled him, too.

He'd found his place, his calling, his people right here in Fairwood, Wyoming.

And he wanted to make it permanent. He was proposing to Caroline tonight. He wanted her to be his wife and Nina to be his daughter.

But was she ready to say yes?

He'd asked Ken to babysit Nina tonight, and he'd told Caroline to dress up and come to his house. She'd be here in a few minutes.

She'd been working on her trust issues and reducing her stress. Yeah, there had been a few angry outbursts—nothing major—and he'd remained calm and held her, and she'd slowly calmed down. And he hadn't been perfect, either. He'd let Nina play too hard a few times without thinking how it affected her glucose. Caroline had forgiven him and moved on without blinking an eye.

They were both works in progress. He wouldn't have it any other way.

The sound of her minivan on the gravel drive sped his pulse. He checked the living room. He'd bought dozens of white roses, turned on romantic music, and he'd put on his Sunday best.

Kylie and Meena had tried to talk him into making a big production out of the proposal, but it wasn't his style. He'd ask her his way. And pray she said yes.

A knock on the door had him closing his eyes briefly. *This is it. God, please let this go well.*

He opened the door, and his mind blanked. She wore a black dress that hugged her curves, drop earrings and black heels.

"Am I too dressed up? We aren't going to Taco Tony's, are we?" She shook her head, her hair caressing her bare shoulders.

"You're stunning. You steal my breath. I…" He blinked, forgetting everything.

"You clean up good, cowboy." Her nose scrunched as she smiled. "What's the plan?"

Plan? Plan. Did he have one? Oh, right.

He took both of her hands in his. "We're not going to Taco Tony's. We're staying here. Sonny prepared a feast for us. It's warming in the oven as we speak."

"Ooh, good, I'm hungry." She turned to go to the eat-in kitchen, but he kept a firm hold on her hands.

"Not so fast. I have something to ask you."

"Are those flowers for me?" She gazed over his shoulder at the vases of roses.

"Yes. But first—"

"They're white. My favorite." She had a dreamy expression.

"That's why I bought them. Now—"

"You didn't have to do that. They're so expensive."

"Caroline." He couldn't prevent sounding exasperated. "Will you listen?"

"Of course. What's up?"

Finally.

"I love you. I'm glad we've been able to spend so much time together over the past months. I feel close to you and Nina."

"I feel close to you, too. And Nina loves you."

"The feeling is mutual. I think it's time we took our relationship to the next level." He bent on one knee and opened the box, presenting it to her. "You're the only woman for me. I love you. I love your lists. I love that you pack a full backpack—just in case—for every outing. I love your pretty smile. I love your notes. And most of all, I love you. I don't want to spend any more time apart. Caroline Bright, will you marry me?"

With eyes gleaming with tears, she nodded rapidly. "Yes. Yes, I'll marry you. I love you, Seth. I want to spend forever with you."

He crushed her to him, savoring her in his arms. Then he looked her in the eyes and kissed her, slowly, deliberately, pouring his heart and soul into it. As she kissed him back, he had no doubts they were meant for each other.

When he ended the kiss, he kept her close.

"I want to adopt Nina." He hoped she wouldn't have a problem with it.

"You'd do that?"

"Yes, I want to."

"Seth, I don't know what to say, but thank you. She'll be the happiest girl in the world. She'll finally have a daddy."

"You've made me the happiest man alive. It's the least I can do for my future daughter."

"You're going to make me cry."

"Caroline, I don't know what I'd do without you. You're the best thing that ever happened to me."

"Seth, you're the best thing that ever happened to me, too."

His heart burst with love. He'd found forever with Caroline, and he couldn't wait to see what the future held.

* * * * *

If you enjoyed this Wyoming Inheritance novel by Jill Kemerer, pick up the first book in the miniseries
The Rancher's Mistletoe Baby
Available now from Love Inspired!

Dear Reader,

I hope you enjoyed this second-chance romance. I got the idea for the book after seeing a post on Instagram about a little girl who had diabetes being helped by a medical alert dog. I can't imagine worrying constantly about such a small child. Caroline and Nina needed Seth and Spud. And Seth and Spud needed them, too.

I confess that, like Caroline, I have my-way-or-the-highway moments. God's grace keeps me relying on Him and setting my stubbornness aside. As for Seth, sometimes in life, we must let go of what's good—a job training service dogs—to embrace what's better: a new career surrounded by loved ones.

Whatever you're facing, please know God loves you. There's nothing that can separate you from His love.

I love connecting with readers. Feel free to contact me at jill@jillkemerer.com or P.O. Box 2802, Whitehouse, Ohio, 43571.

Blessings to you,
Jill Kemerer